Bone

White

Bone White

White

Tim McWhorter

PlotForge, Ltd.

Cover Design by Tim McWhorter
Author Photo by Julie McWhorter
Copyright © 2015 by Tim McWhorter

Published by PlotForge, Ltd.
1650 Lake Shore Drive, Suite 225
Columbus, OH 43204
www.plotforge.com

Bone White
ISBN: 978-1-937979-15-7
Library of Congress Control Number:2015944946

This book is a work of fiction. Names, characters, places and events
portrayed are either the product of the author's imagination or are
used fictitiously. Any resemblance to actual persons, living or dead,
events or locales is entirely coincidental.

Printed in the United States of America

This book is dedicated to Rick and Gary. I couldn't have picked two better friends with whom to share the early chapters of my life. If you look closely throughout this book, you will notice some tips of the hat to those days.

Even though time moves on, and sometimes it seems that all we have left between us are memories, I will cherish and look back on them with a smile for as long as I live.

May our children experience the same level of friendship.

Much love and appreciation goes out to the early readers of this effort. Without their feedback, positive reinforcement, and at times, harsh criticisms, this book would have been much different. And not for the better.
Thank you.

I would also like to thank Terri-Lynne Smiles and the fine people at PlotForge, Ltd. for not only their belief in me and my work, but their enthusiasm for it.

PART I

Whoever is righteous has regard for the life of his beast,
but the mercy of the wicked is cruel.

- Proverbs 12:10

Prologue

10 Years Ago

"Sheriff, you're gonna want to see this."

Deputy Whitaker struggled to keep his voice calm as he spoke into the two-way radio attached at his shoulder. It was like nothing he had ever seen, enough to make his hands tremble. As he stood beside his cruiser, one foot up on the open door jamb, he wiped sweat from his forehead with the red paisley handkerchief his girls had bought him three Christmases ago. Perspiration ran off his face like he was sitting in a sauna, and it wasn't even hot out. When he'd gotten the call to meet with the pastor of the New Congregational Church out on Leads Road, the meteorologist on the early morning news was saying it was going to be the first true day of Autumn-like temperatures. In fact, it couldn't have been more than sixty degrees that stark Monday morning. Yet, even Whitaker's underwear was feeling a little soggy.

"It's a real mess, Sir."

Ten minutes later, Whitaker was sitting in his cruiser with his feet firmly on the ground and his head in his hands when he heard the sound of tires crunching on gravel. He had already lost the cream of wheat, toast and two cups of coffee he'd had for breakfast, and with that caustic taste of vomit lingering in his mouth, had already determined he would be skipping lunch. With a deep breath, Whitaker pulled himself to his feet and watched as Sheriff Stettler's cruiser made its way into the church's parking lot. Another cruiser identical in both color and detail closely followed.

After a wary glance back toward the church, Whitaker walked over to where the Sheriff's car had come to a stop. He had already filled his boss in on what he'd discovered over the radio, but Whitaker knew he'd have to do it all over again. The Sheriff was a stickler for corroboration, even when it came from the same person. The more times you told him a story, the more likely he was to believe and trust in it. And the less likely he was to drown the evidence in a quagmire of reservation.

"Sheriff," Whitaker said, greeting his boss with a nod.

"So, Dick, a real mess, you say?" The Sheriff put on his hat, nestling it down into the indention that had been molded into his thick, greying hair over the years.

"The cellar, sir. Fucking disgusting."

"Well, let's hear it."

"For the last couple weeks," Whitaker started, repeating exactly what he had told the Sheriff ten minutes earlier, "the parishioners have been complaining about a foul odor in the church. After doing some investigating on his own, the pastor narrowed its source as coming from the cellar. Coincidentally, the same cellar that's always kept locked by the church's custodian. Apparently, no one goes down there but him. Insists upon it."

"And the custodian's name?"

"Barnes, sir," Whitaker said. "Corwin James."

"And did you run a preliminary check on this Corwin Barnes?"

"Yes, sir. Came up clean."

"So," the Sheriff started, before taking a moment to spit on the ground, "an all-around upstanding citizen, huh, Dick?"

"Not quite, Sir. Not according to what I found after busting the lock on the cellar door."

Once Deputy Munroe had finally joined them beside Stettler's car, the three officers started the fifty-foot trek across the parking lot toward the church, the soles of their patent leather shoes grating over the gravel.

"Pastor's name is Martin Underwood," Whitaker continued. "Claims Barnes got extremely agitated yesterday when he confronted him after all the church members had gone. Said it would have probably gotten physical had the pastor not walked away. Said Barnes was that agitated."

"So the pastor literally turned the other cheek?" Munroe chimed in from behind. This tickled the Sheriff's funny bone.

"Guess so," Whitaker said, his brow taking on wrinkles. He wasn't in the mood for jokes, and had to remind himself that the only reason Munroe and the sheriff were able to make jokes was because they hadn't yet seen what was in the cellar.

"He didn't know what his rights were," Whitaker continued. "Regarding breaking into the cellar. So he called us."

"And, what did we tell him?" Stettler asked.

"My unofficial answer was, 'it's your church, isn't it?' So I retrieved my bolt cutters from the trunk and we went in. That's where we found it. Or, I guess I should say, where we found *them*." Whitaker's stomach once again turned sour at the thought. Luckily, there was nothing left to come up, so that made it easier to fight off the urge to vomit a second time.

"And where's this pastor now?" the Sheriff asked.

"Inside. Sitting at the top of the stairs. Praying."

When the three lawmen were about halfway to the church's entrance, the double front doors suddenly crashed open with a loud bang, and an older, white haired gentleman burst forth.

"Officer! Officer!"

The pastor rushed down the steps, taking them two at a time before eventually collapsing onto his knees in the narrow strip of manicured grass beside the concrete walkway.

Without hesitation, the three officers rushed over to the hysterical man, with Whitaker arriving a split second earlier than the other two. Kneeling down beside the pastor, Whitaker put a calming hand on the gentleman's quivering shoulder.

"What is it?"

"My God!" the Pastor cried. The palms of his hands rubbed his eyes as if to erase an unsavory image before it had a chance to imprint itself forever on his brain. "There are *three* of them!"

Bone **1** White

Present Day

Just before my fishing line went taut, I noticed the piece of cloth floating in the pool of shimmering sunlight, reflecting on the water like gold foil. Drifting about fifteen feet off the bow of the boat, it rode the lake's gentle currents without any clear destination. Floating aimlessly. Just lost.

Kind of how my father would describe me.

I cranked the handle on my new Shimano reel a couple more times and watched the end of my fiberglass pole arc farther downward with each turn. The arc only bent sharper when I tried to pull up on the rod. Like a plucked guitar string, the greenish-tinged monofilament line only vibrated, cutting short jagged slices through the water's surface. It didn't matter whether I cranked or pulled; the line remained firm and unrelenting. Whatever was on the other end, it was certainly not a fish. There was no independent movement. No fighting back and forth. Only solid, unchanging rigidness. Whatever it was, it wasn't about to budge.

"What's up, Luke?" Garrett asked through pursed lips, his own fishing line held between them as he tied on a new hook.

"Don't know," I answered. "Guess I'm snagged on something."

"Alright, gimme a sec."

The early light of the day was still chasing the mist from the water's surface as we floated about thirty feet off a rocky shore, hovering over a well-known drop-off in the lakebed. It was a lazy Saturday, and according to the fish finder, there was supposedly nothing below us but a few fish. Nothing I should be hooked on.

But the fish finder had been wrong before.

I gave the line another tug or two before scrambling to my feet for better leverage. Pressing my knee against the side of the aluminum boat, I steadied myself against the roll and sway, which promised to only get worse the more I fought the line. As any experienced fisherman knows, when you get a snag, there's a fine line between pulling just enough to free it, and pulling so hard it breaks the line, so I pulled only as hard as I dared.

Garrett appeared with a wooden oar in his hands, like he was prepared for battle. He struck a pose for either a camera or a group of girls, neither of which was anywhere in sight. Then, laughing it off like he meant to look like an idiot, he plunged the paddle end of the oar into the water and jabbed at whatever he could make contact with. The oar bumped against the line from time to time but it wasn't creating any slack. After a couple of minutes of poking and prodding, I was just as snagged up as when he started. I glanced over to see if the piece of cloth was still there while I waited. It was. It could be a shirt. Maybe blue.

"It's not giving at all," Garrett said, bumping it again with the oar. "I just hope it's not a, you know, dead body or anything."

I knew he meant it as a joke, but the comment hung in the crisp, early morning air, both of us knowing its reference all too well. On the ride to the lake the night before, I counted road kill passing through the truck's headlights when I was awake. But, when I dozed, I dreamed about Megan Bradshaw and Hannah Rogers, the two girls missing from our high school, disappeared without a trace.

Just gone.

"I think I can feel the bottom," Garrett said as he continued to jab at the water, arms elbow-deep, ass in the air. "Fairly shallow right here."

"Maybe try and dig at it."

Missing teenagers were something new around here. Something our small town of 1,600 had never dealt with before. And no one could tell us exactly what to do, or how to act. Suspicion became the norm, and we saw shadows where there were none. Pieces of trash along the roadside became dumped bodies just waiting to be discovered. Anything out of the ordinary turned our thoughts in the direction of the missing girls, trying to determine if there was a connection. And that was reason number one why I hadn't just cut both my losses and my fishing line by now. A four-dollar lure wasn't worth the amount of time and effort we were spending on what was normally a routine snag. But, like everything else that was no longer routine, we both wanted to know what had ahold of my line, what rested at the bottom of the lake. It was a stretch for sure, thinking that maybe I had snagged onto a dead body. Chances were really good that it was anything but. However, like I said, suspicion had become the norm.

Garrett got to his feet and put all his weight onto the handle of the oar, plunging the wide end into the muddy bottom of the lake until the oar was almost completely submerged. Bubbles in various shades of brown began rising to the surface like volcanoes erupting from the deep.

My hands were starting to cramp from keeping the line tight, and I took a moment to flex one hand, while still holding firm with the other. Despite not yet knowing what was down there in the murky water, I found myself nearing my "screw it, just cut it" point.

"Maybe you should jump in and feel around," I taunted.

"Maybe you should kiss my ass," Garrett said. The look he gave me said it was the stupidest suggestion I had ever made. He was just worried about what he might bump into in the water, because honestly, I'd said things that were far more stupid. I was sure of it.

I looked again at the piece of cloth riding the ripples given off by the listing boat. It was closer now and a shirt for sure. Dark blue. And it gave me the chills. Despite my best efforts to ignore the discarded garment, my imagination spewed forth questions. What was a shirt doing floating out in the middle of the lake anyway? A rag, maybe. A handkerchief, I could see. Hell, even a jacket would have made more sense. But, a shirt? Most people would notice they'd lost a shirt. Unless of course, that someone had had no say in—

A sucking sound jolted my back straight. I felt it as much as heard it as the pressure on the rod eased. My heart pounded as I knew we would soon see what had held my line hostage for so long. The arc of the rod grew less severe. Less of an arc, and more of a slight bend for the first time since I'd gotten the snag. Like an opportunistic used car salesman, I immediately started reeling in the line.

"Yes!" Garrett said, sitting back and taking a breather. "Finally."

The line was coming up alright, but coming up slowly. There was still enough tension on the line for the reel's drag to occasionally make its clicking sound. I was working hard, too hard for the little amount of line I was bringing in.

"It's comin," I said, "but it feels like there's something heavy on the other end. Somethin' really heavy."

Like dead weight.

We exchanged a quick glance, and I was glad I hadn't voiced my thought. Still, the look was enough to tell us we knew what the other was thinking. I couldn't stop my mind from delving further toward thoughts I really didn't want to have. And conclusions I didn't want to come to. I rushed to come up with other possible scenarios, anything else my line could have hooked into besides a dead body. But, it was too late. The image was already in my head. So all I could do was brace myself for whatever was to come and just keep cranking.

Garrett scowled and cautiously knelt beside me. Proving he was still braver than me, he leaned over and put his face down near the water to get a better look, rocking the boat slightly as he did. Unfortunately, all the digging he had done with the oar had churned the mud and turned the water a murky brown.

I slowly cranked the handle on the reel, bringing the line in little by little. The seconds ticked by at the pace of minutes as we waited impatiently for whatever was on the other end of the line to show itself. For the lake to reveal what was on its bottom. To give up its secret.

Click...click...click...

The surface broke as a long, thin hand reached up toward Garrett's face. Its flesh was gone, leaving behind only twisted, black bones. When the fingertips brushed his cheek, Garrett leapt backward with an audible shriek. Landing ass first on the floor of the boat, an errant elbow sending my tackle box tumbling. Hooks, weights, spinners and plastic worms of every color scattered all over the worn grey carpeting of the boat.

The fishing pole began to slip from my grip as I reared back to escape the ghoulish menace when just as quickly, it changed into something less so. As soon as it emerged further, the bony hand transformed into its true form; a simple tree branch, black with age and algae. Submerged for who knows how long, its gnarled and crooked limbs vaguely resembled the charred bones of a skeleton. The small twigs branching out at the end took on the illusion of fingers, all the way down to the knobby knuckles. If I hadn't still been in shock, I would have busted out laughing. No tree branch in history had ever looked so sinister, or instilled so much fear. But, as it was, all I could do was stand there processing, surprised at the quickness with which we'd jumped to conclusions.

I looked at Garrett. The first thing I saw in his eyes was recognition. Then, a welcome relief spread across his face like a tidal wave, bringing with it an awkward grin. Meeting my gaze from where he sat, legs in the air, I'm sure he saw the same on mine. Like I said, having two girls missing from the area made you skittish. It caused you to jump to conclusions, even when it seemed like a ridiculous notion afterward. I'm sure it didn't help that we'd also seen too many horror movies. At least that's what my mother would have said. And she would know. She knows everything.

Once our testicles had dropped out of our stomachs and we'd finally had a good laugh about it all, we went ahead and cut the line. We watched in silence as, slowly, the tree limb sank back down and returned to its resting place under the murky water where it had resided for who knows how long before being disturbed. I looked across the water, and the blue shirt too, was gone. If that's even what it was. Now, I couldn't be sure.

The sun had risen over the horizon during our battle with the branch, the mist was almost gone and the world around us was gradually coming into focus. We'd been fishing all night and the gods had been good to us, so we decided not to be greedy. Besides, we were running out of space in the cooler.

"Next weekend?" Garrett asked.

"Definitely."

Garrett turned the boat in the direction of the launch ramp and his awaiting truck. After haphazardly tossing the spilled gear into the tackle box to be sorted later, I kicked my feet up on the bow of the boat for the ride back. With the sun now blazing down upon us, I pulled my hat down over my eyes, but not before glimpsing a trio of vultures circling high in the blue sky above, their long, black wings spread wide against the ice blue backdrop.

I had once read that the site of vultures circling overhead was regarded as a bad omen, but I didn't consider it one at the time.

But, maybe I should have.

Bone **2** White

The next week was mostly normal. School during the day, working my job in the evenings, and filling the in-between time with more of the unwavering tension between my parents and me regarding my plans for the future, or the lack thereof. We were like broken records. I would tell them that I didn't know what I wanted to do after high school, and my parents would lecture me on the dangers of idle hands. In other words, that week was no different from the ones that had come before.

Well, with the exception of Becca Lewis disappearing.

Bone 3 White

New Paris, Ohio, is a dual stoplight town situated just inside the Ohio/Indiana border, no closer to a big city than it has to be. It's the kind of town where the population of the cemeteries exceed that of the living, and the gap seems to widen every year. We have a McDonald's and one of those Summer, roadside ice cream stands that sells things like pizza burgers and deep fried mushrooms, things you can't get anywhere except places like that. We have a rundown carwash, more churches than bars, and a post office that's only open when our local postmaster can pull himself out of the latter. It's a place where families go back several generations, and the chaotic world we see on the nightly news might as well be on another planet.

It's not the kind of town where disappearances occur.

But, in a matter of six weeks, three teenage girls had gone missing. I knew each of them. In a town the size of New Paris, everyone pretty much knows everyone else. Rumors flew through the air the way pigeons scatter in the movies when couples stroll through the town square. Meaning, there were a lot of them flying in all directions, and you just had to try and stay out of their way, all the while covering your head and trying not to get shit on. The rumors morphed from one telling to the next, always growing the way rumors often do.

One rumor I'd heard had the girls belonging to a suicide cult that planned a suicide every other week until there were no girls left in New Paris. While not exactly a far-fetched notion, in my mind at least, this theory didn't actually explain the physical disappearances of the girls. But, that didn't seem to matter to the individuals spreading the rumor. They just gave me a dumb look and walked away when I pointed it out.

Coincidentally or not, all three of the missing girls were part of the elite clique, and yes, even small towns have those. The pretty rich girls who weren't necessarily snobs, but had the DNA to be one if the mood struck. That gave wings to another rumor flying around suggesting they'd all run away for the bright lights of Los Angeles or New York or Nashville. Led off into the dark night, guided only by the stars in their eyes.

I'd even heard a rumor that all three were chained up somewhere in the bowels of the high school, kept there by our 7-fingered school janitor who may or may not have served time in prison at one point. As time went on, it seemed like each rumor offered a more outlandish explanation than the last.

As for me, I didn't know what I believed.

The mood was somber at lunch on that following Thursday as Garrett and I, and a handful of others gathered on and around his tailgate, a bag of cheeseburgers between us in the crowded McDonald's parking lot. We were all thinking about the same thing. The missing students were all *anyone* around town could think about. Sometimes we even caught ourselves looking at girls in the school hallways, wondering who would be next. Which one of them was going to off themselves this week? Who had their bags packed and a bus ticket in hand? Or, who wasn't taking an alternate route to their classes in order to avoid walking past the janitor's closet?

"Maybe they're all just playing a trick," Cricket said, breaking a silence almost five minutes long, which among a group of people my age is a long freakin' time. "Like a hoax, or something. To get themselves on television." His real name was Sukhraj Singh, but we called him Cricket. We told ourselves it was because the baseball-like sport was all he ever talked about after his family moved here from Mumbai. But, admittedly, it was also a whole lot easier to pronounce than "Sukhraj" without sounding like we were mocking him. Cricket held the distinction of being the only Indian kid in our high school. In fact, his family was practically the only non-white family in town. The PC officers of the world wouldn't exactly call New Paris 'multi-cultural.' Cricket's family moved to town two years ago when his father was given the responsibility of heading up some kind of rehabilitation program at the prison on the other side of the county. Not sure what he did exactly, but it had something to do with helping the convicts transition better into society after they were released. Something with an acronym for a name. He'd joined up with Garrett and me pretty quick and had been hanging with us ever since. Cricket that is, not his father. Cricket never went fishing with us, though. Couldn't pull him away from YouTube and World of Warcraft long enough. But, he was a good guy. And his mother made some really tasty food that was a whole lot easier to eat than pronounce.

"Really?" Garrett asked him with more than a hint of sarcasm. He was on edge as much as any of us, if not more. He had a sister who was a freshman this year. Of the three missing girls, two were seniors and one was a junior. Still, you never know. "Do you really think they're just playing a trick?"

The look on Cricket's face told me he'd taken Garrett's sarcasm too personally. The corners of his mouth turned downward a bit. His light dimmed.

"Well, no," Cricket said, his eyes down at his feet as he slurped his milkshake. "Just tryin' to stay positive, I guess."

Cricket looked up at me for solidarity sake, and I gave him props with a nod. Staying positive was something very few people in town were succeeding at, so I had to at least give him credit for trying.

"The cops have practically nothing," Garrett continued. His aunt was married to one of the four deputy sheriffs in New Paris, so we knew he spoke the truth on that topic. "Even the FBI hasn't made any headway. What are we supposed to make of that?"

His question was met with modest shrugs and bowed heads. None of us had any idea what we were supposed to make of any of it. So we just stuffed our faces with cheeseburgers, fries and milkshakes in the hopes we wouldn't be asked our opinions directly.

"Annabeth Wilson wasn't in History this morning," Claire eventually said, before tossing a couple of fries into her mouth. Claire was the token "one-of-the-guys" girl in our little group, what my mother called 'a tomboy.' She wasn't into fishing, but she was a very good basketball player, a so-so volleyball player and served time on both teams in school. Claire hung with us instead of other girls, basically because a lot of the other girls thought she was a lesbian, and just like with diversity, acceptance wasn't our town's strong suit. But, the girls at school were wrong anyway. I knew this because Claire and I had made out more than a couple times. But, no one else knew about it, and we were generally content to keep it a secret. Not like it would have mattered to the rest of our group either way. Gay or straight, she was just plain cool.

"Anyone seen her?" Claire continued.

The shaking of heads silently confirmed that none of us had seen Annabeth. More than likely, she just had a headache, stomachache or at worst, a case of mono. Really, there could have been any number of reasons why she wasn't in class. Maybe she simply had an exam that day and hadn't had a chance to study. So instead of getting a bad grade, she just chose to skip. Who knows? Kids had skipped classes for a lot less. But, that's how it worked lately: if a girl wasn't in class, we held our breaths until she showed up somewhere.

And that's how Garrett and I spent the rest of the week; holding our breath, fearing the worst and looking forward to our weekend of fishing just so we'd get a break from it all.

Bone 4 White

Just before the final Friday bell, the principal came on the loud speaker and wished us all a good weekend. After reminding us of the school board's decision to go ahead with prom that was two weeks away, he signed off with his usual "Can't wait to see everyone on Monday." Only this time, he made a point of telling us to be careful, that he wouldn't want anything to happen to any more of "his students."

In any other school across the country, that would have seemed like an awkward thing to say. Normally, when the principal or a teacher made a seemingly odd statement, I rolled my eyes or smirked. Maybe mocked them outright in order to get a laugh. This time, I let it go. I gathered my books and walked quietly out of the classroom as the bell rang through the hallways for the last time.

Incidentally, Annabeth was back in school that day. A simple 24-hour stomach virus had kept her home the day before. Rumor had it, though, that she'd eaten some bad Mexican food the night before and it had given her the squirts. But, that's how rumors go, and hers was just one of many flying around.

Bone 5 White

Friday nights, it was usually assholes and elbows for Garrett at the steakhouse where we both worked as dishwashers. I'd have been right there with him had I not thrown a fit awhile back and said my mom was threatening to report them for making me work too many hours at my age. From that point on, I had my Friday nights free. Unfortunately for Garrett, I'd thought of it first.

But, by some grace of God, or just dumb luck, Garrett didn't have to work that night. The steakhouse had hired a new dishwasher, and, finally, Garrett had actual seniority over someone. That meant we could get a much desired early start for the lake. Even though we usually fished mostly at night, it was easier to launch the boat and get out on the water while the sun was still up. Adding all the tension in my house with my parents, and the all-around uneasiness running rampant through New Paris, I was all too eager to make myself scarce. Besides, the lingering rain that week only added to the melancholic atmosphere that hovered over New Paris with all the subtlety of a zeppelin on fire. Getting away for the next twenty-four hours was just what we needed, and we couldn't get out of town soon enough.

This is what Garrett and I did. We fished. Loved it. It's what we lived for, and what made us different from most the kids we knew. When the rest of our senior class made plans to spend their Spring Breaks in Myrtle Beach or Daytona, Garrett and I headed northeast. We packed our gear and spent the week trout fishing up in the Allegheny National Forest in northern Pennsylvania. My father, for one, thought we were crazy for choosing trout fishing and a rundown cabin in the woods over bikinis and sand, but what can I say? There's just something about the freedom and being in nature that draws us in. When Sunday evenings came along and Garrett's blue Chevy truck smelled like mud, fish attractant and spilled Mtn Dew, we considered it a good weekend. If the cooler happened to be full of bass, catfish or a whole mess of perch, then we considered it a *very* good weekend.

That Friday, Garrett swung by my house wearing the faded green Master Baiter t-shirt he'd found online a few years back. The picture on the back showed a small, but muscular, guy in shades wrestling a monster worm onto a hook. It was classic Garrett. He rounded out his angling "uniform" with cargo shorts and old tennis shoes. Basically, it was the same thing I was wearing except for the shirt. My grey t-shirt had a simple Bass Pro Shop logo on the pocket. Nothing fancy.

We pulled out of the driveway around 5:00, about twenty minutes before my parents would be home, robbing them of the chance to ask a ton of questions the way they did when they thought I spent too much time doing something useless, and not enough time doing what they thought I should be. I left a simple note on the fridge telling them we were going to siesta at the lake overnight and not to expect me home until sometime the following afternoon. I wouldn't be getting away scot-free, though. My mother always insisted I called at some point in the evening, anytime I stayed somewhere overnight. So, I had that to look forward to.

I'm not sure if it was the stress of the week or the prospect of a good catch on account of the rain, but Garrett was more excited than usual to get the hell out of Dodge. He pushed the old truck just a little faster. The engine roared like a beast, and I felt the vibration of a much needed wheel alignment under my feet. In the side mirror, I saw the trailer bouncing along behind us, jumping the tiny dips in the worn out back roads the way I'd seen boats do when they raced on TV. With Jason Aldean's "Dirt Road Anthem" appropriately coming at us from the truck's tinny door speakers, our moods that afternoon were starting to lighten. We could breathe. The week was finally over. We were free for two whole days, and New Paris, with its growing paranoia, was in the rearview mirror, shrinking in the distance with every hill the old pickup rambled over.

We were at the launch ramp, removing the canvas covering from the boat, when Garrett brought it up – the topic of my parents and the pressure they'd been putting on me. He knew I didn't want to talk about it, but that's how Garrett was. Always looking out for me. Always trying to help.

"You know they're right," he said, coiling the yellow nylon rope between his hand and elbow. "Graduation's in a few weeks. Then what?" It was easy for Garrett to side with my parents; his future had been planned out the minute the red Hoover & Son sign went up over the old auto garage on Bishop Street. Garrett was just five years old at the time. He was gung-ho about it though, and had sole-proprietorship stars in his eyes. His decision or not, that was his future. Mine, as my parents had been reminding me lately, was still up in the air. What was I going to do after high school? College? I was already long overdue in checking into any schools. Work? The discussion was like the astronomical layout at night, perpetually the same. It usually started with my mother, only she wouldn't come out and say it. She would start with, "Luke, your father and I…" But, it was part of her routine to stop somewhere around there and let her words hover in the room. At some point, my father would eventually notice the hanging silence from behind his laptop screen and recognize it as his cue. He'd bluntly, if not eloquently, finish my mother's sentence with, "you need to get your head out of the clouds and start making some decisions. Take charge of your life." But, it wasn't that I hadn't been thinking about it. I truly didn't know what I wanted to do with my life. Who knows? Maybe Garrett would hire me to turn wrenches at his garage.

Rolling up the grey nylon tarp we used as a boat cover, I felt the first breath of a cool, damp breeze. It wasn't a full-on gust, but just enough to bristle the tiny hairs on the back of my neck. I used it to my advantage. An opportunity to change the subject.

"Better grab our jackets," I said, just before a shiver rippled my back. Twice.

Forgetting the previous conversation, momentarily at least, Garrett cast his eyes skyward while tossing the coil of rope into the bed of the truck. "Yep. Looks like something might be blowing in."

And it did. While we spent the next half hour cruising around the lake looking for a good spot, or at least what the fish finder told us would be a good spot, the wind picked up considerably, and the clouds moved in. Dark, menacing clouds, the color of gunmetal, rolled across the sky in a slow moving wave, blanketing it from one horizon to the other.

Uneasiness creeping into my mood, I pulled out the new cell phone I had bought with my last two paychecks, intent on checking the weather forecast. But, no matter how I held the phone, I couldn't get service out where we were. The webpage would start to load, only to get stuck somewhere between opening fully and flipping me the bird.

"Any luck?"

"Nah," I said, slipping the useless phone back into my jacket pocket. "Too far from civilization, I guess."

Garrett smiled as he throttled up the boat's motor.

"Good. That's exactly where we want to be."

Bone **6** White

It was an impossible choice. This time, Garrett was royally screwed either way. There was no easy out. My friends and I sometimes played the "Would You Rather" game. The idea is to offer up two completely messed up choices, and your friend has to choose which scenario they'd rather endure even though they really don't want to do either. And I mean *really*. That's how you know you picked good scenarios. The one I had just given Garrett was worthy of the Would You Rather Hall of Fame, if someone had the foresight to organize such a thing.

"Damn, Luke, that's sick," Garrett said, his face squinched up like he'd just smelt one he hadn't dealt. As he looked out over the water at nothing in particular, I could tell he was running both scenarios in his head and thanking God that this was just a game. "Where the hell'd you come up with that one?"

I smiled proudly.

"I thought of it in Richardson's class this afternoon," I said. Health class was generally a great source of "Would You Rather" choices.

"I don't wanna do either," he said, before feigning a gagging sound and clutching his stomach.

We were slowly trolling along the southeastern bank of the lake, about 300 yards from the dam. Garrett was in the back steering the boat, and I was in my usual spot up front in the bow. The sky was still churning shades of grey, but so far had held off spitting any rain down upon us. But, that's the only luck we were having. When you're out fishing, a single bite in almost an hour leads you to start playing games like Would You Rather.

"Come on, man, you gotta pick one," I goaded as I cast out my line. "Would you rather walk in on your parents having sex, or have to drink your own urine to survive?" Now, the last thing teenagers want to think about is their parents having sex. But, to actually catch them in the act? That was everyone's worst nightmare come true. Nobody wants to see their dad's hairy ass bobbing up and down as he's putting it to the saintly woman who brought you into the world.

"Where would I be that I'd have to drink my own urine?"

"I don't know," I said, slowly reeling in a neon green spinner bait. "Lost at sea. Stranded in the desert, maybe."

We continued trolling the bank in a westward direction toward the dam. The shoreline in the area was rough and rocky. Ten to twelve foot cliffs dropped out of the sky, straight down to the water. A rich, dark earth mixed with a little clay was exposed. Up on top, there was nothing but lush, green trees as far and as deep as you could see. Spring's hard work was paying off, and the lake was certainly the peaceful seclusion we had been anticipating all week.

"Well, I'd rather drink *my own* urine than someone else's," he said, firing up the motor to head somewhere that might be more fruitful. "Does that count?"

"Only if you're taking the urine drinking option," I said as I sat there smiling, waiting patiently for his answer. Knowing Garrett's parents the way I did, I had a feeling I knew which way he was going to go. To hear his sister talk, Garrett's parents still did it routinely, and I knew the possibility of one of the scenarios actually happening was playing through Garrett's mind. Which explained the pained look on his face.

Then, the scenarios were suddenly forgotten as the boat started shaking violently, and the motor started making a loud chugging sound.

"Shit!" Garrett cursed. He let his fishing rod drop against the white vinyl seat and made a mad grab for the black hood of the boat's motor.

"What's up?" I asked, but then I saw it. The churning water behind the boat swirled with various shades of brown. Long strands of dark green and caramel-colored kelp rose to the surface. We'd run aground in a shallow area of the lake.

Not good.

Garrett shut off the motor and tilted it forward, bringing the propeller up out of the water.

"Shit," I heard him say again. "Shit. Shit. Shit."

I looked over his shoulder as the profanities echoed back to us from the cliffs, and instantly saw what had brought them on. Where the propeller should have had three blades, there were now only two. A jagged edge, like a toothless grin, was all that remained where the third blade had once been. We'd snapped it off when we'd run shallow. *Really* not good. A shiver went through me, either from the increasing wind or the suddenness of how quickly our circumstances had changed. More than likely, a combination of both.

"Great," I said, casting a glance up at an angry sky. "Now what?"

"Well," Garrett said, standing with one hand on his hip and the other rubbing his temple. "We're sure as hell not gonna make it back with this." Then, in an uncharacteristic move, he kicked the top of the motor just above the Mercury nameplate.

I looked in the direction of the launch ramp, but couldn't even see it. We were a good three or four miles away, and it was getting dark. I remember Garrett saying at one time that it would be a good idea to pick up a spare prop just for situations like this. Leave it stored away on the boat. But, I could tell by the way he was acting that he never got around to it.

"That's a hell of a long way to swim."

"You ain't kiddin'," he said, balancing himself as the boat gently rocked back and forth. "And this wind is only pushing us farther away. Better drop that anchor. At least until we figure out a plan."

I got down on my knees and reached into the cubbyhole of the boat's bow. I pulled out a coil of dirty, fraying rope that used to be white, but was now the color of dirty dishwater. On one end of the rope was an anchor we'd made out of a large coffee can simply by filling it with concrete. I dropped the can over the side and let the rope slide smoothly through my hands as it made its way to the bottom. Awhile back, we'd put black electrical tape on the rope at one-foot intervals. That way we could count them as the rope disappeared, and would know exactly how deep the water was wherever we were. This time, once the can had eventually settled on the muddy bottom and the rope had stopped retreating, seven rings of tape had disappeared. Seven feet. That wasn't good. The lower unit of the boat's motor extended below the water's surface by about eighteen inches. So the water below us being seven feet deep meant that the wind had already blown the boat away from where we'd hit bottom only a minute ago. And blown us that much further from the warmth and safety of Garrett's truck.

Bone 7 White

As we heaved the front end of the aluminum boat up onto a small stretch of sandy shore, lightning splintered the roiling sky off in the distance. It was a miracle we'd happened onto the oasis hidden among the sheer cliffs and rocky lakeshore. Turns out, not only was it our best option, but it was our only option. The homemade anchor had proved no match for the freight train-like wind. Despite the concrete-filled coffee can's best efforts, the gusts were still blowing the boat toward the shoreline, dragging the anchor across the bottom. The anchor may as well have not even been there.

Likewise, the oars we had on hand didn't serve us much better. After wasting several torturous minutes and an unknown amount of energy trying to paddle against the current, we found that our best strategy was to simply use the oars to help steer toward this sandy part of the shoreline and away from the large rocks. Eventually, when it appeared as if the wind was intent on carrying us past even the small beach, we got out in waist deep water and waded the last ten yards.

Struggling to hold the boat against the wind and waves was like trying to fly a 300 pound metal kite. With every gust, the boat swayed in all directions except the one we wanted. Two-foot waves pounded us every step of the way, filling my mouth with lake water more than once. But, in the end, we battled through and won the war.

As we hauled the boat up onto the shore, its heavy V-hull bottom sliced deep into the sand. It tilted to one side as whitecaps curled their way onto land, beating against the back and sides of the vessel. After a brief debate, we determined there was enough of the boat out of the water to keep it in place, or at least keep it from floating away. That was our hope anyway, since there was nothing to tie off to on the empty stretch of beach. Still, before we walked away, Garrett pulled the boat up another couple inches just for good measure.

We gathered up a few of our belongings and secured everything else against the raging wind. We didn't worry too much about anyone stealing anything since we hadn't seen anyone on the lake all evening. Or on shore, for that matter. No one in their right minds should have been out in that weather. Apparently, Garrett and I were the only ones who hadn't gotten the memo regarding the forecast. As nice as we'd thought it would be to get away, I would have chosen to stay in town and play World of Warcraft with Cricket rather than being cold, wet and stranded.

"Something wicked this way comes," Garrett said in his scariest of voices, while gazing up at the ever-darkening sky. We'd read the Bradbury classic in our 11th grade Lit class. It was okay. I'm not much of a reader, and a lot of what we'd read had to be explained to me. But, like a lot of things in life that you have to endure and just get through, I got through that book and subsequently, the class. Garrett, on the other hand, enjoyed the book thoroughly and quoted it often. Sometimes the title was enough.

Dark and angry clouds churned above us in every shade of grey known to man. I knew it wouldn't be long now. And as soon as the thought entered my mind, I felt the first drops.

"Looks like wicked's already here," I said.

Soaked from our shoulders down, we left the openness of the beach and trudged through a narrow half-sand, half-gravel path that led over the rocky embankment. We had to duck our way under low-lying tree limbs that would occasionally reach out and grab our jackets if we didn't crouch low enough, as if they were trying to stop us from going any further, or punish us for even being there in the first place. Once out of the trees, we still had to scramble over a collection of Fiat-sized boulders with deep crevices between them, risking both twisted ankles and bruised knees.

Finally, we reached the other side of the embankment, and hurdled a rusted steel guardrail to a not so recently paved parking lot. There was room for five or six cars to park, though currently, the lot was empty except for an overflowing trashcan. A crinkled fast food bag hung out of the can's opening that made it look like it was sticking a tongue out at us. Taunting us. On the ground beside the can, a cardboard box full of empty beer bottles lay tipped over on its side. It wasn't clear how close the litterer had gotten to the trashcan before hurling the box in its direction, but a few of the bottles didn't survive the toss.

Thunder rumbled overhead and large drops of rain hit the ground around us, making tiny splat sounds as they met the pavement. Not a full-on downpour yet, but it was working its way up to one nice and slow, like the storm was toying with us until it grew tired of the game and really wanted to flex some muscle on a couple of punk kids who should have known better than to be out.

Better hurry!

I zipped up my jacket, and without any unnecessary discussion, we started across the abandoned parking lot. There were no other options. No gas stations where we could use the phone. No internet cafes where we could even send an email or instant message. We utilized the little bit of remaining light to sidestep broken glass, blue Styrofoam bait containers and more than one used condom. By all appearances, the empty parking lot wasn't always this vacant. Just tonight.

Lucky us.

A tree-lined road led us out and away from the lot where the asphalt pavement of the road was just as old, pitted and broken in places. Grooves were worn into it where cars had continually driven on the soft and bubbly asphalt during scorching summers. Judging by the trash in the parking lot, the road was still in use, just not enough to justify doing any real maintenance to it. It proved bad enough that we found it easier to walk in the tall, wet grass, rather than on the road itself.

As the lake and remaining daylight fell farther behind us, the smell of new rain mixed with pine and rot soon filled our nostrils. It hung heavy in the cooling air, replacing the dropping humidity as acres of trees walled us in on both sides. Evergreens and any number of others that Garrett would have had little trouble identifying in the daylight made up the most of it. Occasionally, there were tall, barren trees that hadn't come back in the Spring, stretching up into the evening sky like the walking sticks of giants. In the diminished light, I could only see a few feet into the thick woods. Cutting through these woods, in the dark, was officially crossed off my list of plans for finding shelter. It was just going be us and the road, no matter where it led.

As the parking lot and all its debris fell completely out of sight, the rain started coming down harder, pelting our skin.

Stinging it. Like it was trying to break through. And all we could do was walk.

Bone **8** White

"I think I'd rather drink my own urine."

"Really?" I said, letting out the first laugh I'd managed in half an hour. It was the first reason I'd had, to say the least. We were soaked from head to toe, shivering like Chihuahuas, and with every step, I was growing surer and surer we were the only people in whatever county this was.

"Yeah," Garrett said, loud enough to be heard over the wind and rain. "I've heard of people having to do that before, so it must work. And if it meant staying alive..."

The conversation went on like that for awhile as we walked along the abandoned road that seemingly led nowhere. Ten minutes had passed. Then twenty. Still, we'd seen no houses. No cars had come along. No signs of civilization, period. Only trees and more trees. And with the rain still coming down on us like an unrelenting attack dog, we needed something to take our minds off the fact that we were smack dab in the middle of some pretty screwed up circumstances. And if that something was Garrett's urine, then so be it. Hell, I'd be happy to talk about it all night long.

Luckily, though, that wasn't necessary. We'd probably walked a good mile or two when we finally came upon a private driveway, its gravel long since pulverized into dust. The rain was transforming a pothole that stretched from one side of the driveway's mouth to the other, into a muddy swimming pool. It would have probably swallowed up most economy cars if they'd tried to take it on. Tall weeds surrounded the entrance on both sides, and wilted brown ivy snaked its way up two crooked, black lampposts that were posted like crippled sentries of a surrendering castle. They remained dutifully at their post, despite the loss of their charge.

I knew my low-budget slasher flicks, and every one I'd ever seen flashed through my mind. Unimaginatively, most started with a group of college kids looking for somewhere to party and have unprotected sex. Emphasis on the "unprotected" part, because, in those movies at least, they rarely survived the sex. Insert public service announcement here.

"Jesus," I mumbled, staring down the winding driveway that seemed to have no end. Tree limbs on both sides created a tunnel that went on forever, and the dirt drive simply dissolved into the shadows with it.

"Yeah," Garrett said. "I bet there's a house with a phone at the other end."

Did I mention that besides being the brains of our little group, Garrett was also the one with the biggest balls? Skeletal hands rising out of a murky lake notwithstanding, I had rarely ever seen him scared of anything. I, on the other hand, was his opposite. Along with clowns and insects larger than my thumb, a dark and foreboding forest rounded out the trio of things that meant nightmares for me.

"Hey, uh, I didn't say 'Jesus' like it was a good thing," I said, my head pivoting back and forth. "It was more of a 'Jesus, this place looks really creepy and we should probably just keep walking.' "

Garrett was already shaking his head and smirking. He knew my fears. But, he also knew his power of persuasion over me was second to none. If I wanted to steer clear of whatever was at the other end of the driveway, I had to talk fast.

"Look, I don't know where it leads," I continued, practically shouting over the rain. "And I don't wanna know. Let's just keep goin'. I mean, seriously."

The words had barely escaped my lips when the sky opened up, as if Mother Nature herself had decide to chide me for my cowardice. Heavy rain fell in torrents, literally stinging the top of my uncovered head. Cats and dogs had nothing on these raindrops. In no time, a world-class thunderstorm was beating us down, growing more intense by the minute, and adding more weight behind Garrett's argument for checking out the driveway.

"Come on," Garrett urged, pulling the drawstring tighter on his red-hooded jacket and making me resent that mine didn't have one. "We don't have much choice. We have to get out of this nasty shit. At the very least, there's got to be some kind of house back there. Some kind of shelter, at least. They don't just put in random driveways because they think they'll add to the natural beauty of things."

He had to shout, even though I was standing right beside him. That's how bad it was coming down. And that's how I knew that Garrett was right. We didn't have much choice. Continuing to walk all night in this weather was neither a pleasant nor compelling alternative. It could be miles before we saw another driveway and we needed to ride this storm out somewhere.

Garrett looked at me and must have seen what he wanted, because he simply grinned and started walking down the driveway without me, skirting the mud hole that was starting to look more like a small pond at that point. Still, there was hesitation in my step. I lagged behind, dragging my feet like an angry toddler. It wasn't until a brilliant display of lightning, followed by an ear-piercing crack of thunder propelled me to follow more swiftly in Garrett's footsteps.

Bone 9 White

Have you ever been gripped with fear, only to find that not only were your fears unjustified, but the very thing you feared turned out to be a positive thing? That's how I felt after entering the canopied driveway. Despite my initial hesitancy to enter the tunnel of trees, it didn't take long before we were reaping the benefits of our decision. The canopy blocked the wind and diverted most of the rainwater before it ever got to us. The shelter from the relentless storm calmed the uneasiness churning in the pit of my stomach, though it didn't stop me from looking over my shoulder toward the entrance of the driveway and the ever-disappearing road. Outside the tunnel, the wind still howled, the thunder still clapped and the lightning still lit up the night. The only effect it had on us was when the wind really kicked up and slapped the branches aside just enough to infiltrate our cover. Then it would reach us, but only briefly. A few drops of water dripped off the overhead mash, finding their way through from time to time. But that was it. I actually felt safer among the trees, and for the most part, out of the elements.

Still, it was creepy dark inside the tunnel, darker by a few shades, and if there was one downfall, that was it. The shadows were more dreadful inside, the depth of the murkiness between the trees deeper. But, I also recognized that nightfall was descending all around us anyway, so I didn't hold the trees accountable.

Just before we lost the last bit of light, Garrett tugged on my arm and nodded toward a small hill on his side of the driveway.

"There's something over there."

My eyes searched the darkness for what he'd been nodding at, surprised he had seen anything in the low light.

"What do you think it is?" I asked.

The matter of fact shrug I got in return told me it was a dumb question.

"Only one way to find out."

We started up the hill that was slippery from the little bit of rain that was dripping from overhead. The hill was covered with more raw earth than actual grass, most likely because little sunlight ever broke through the natural awning above, so the dirt was slowly turning to mud. My tennis shoes weren't doing well with it. The brown sludge caked the soles, stripping away all traction.

When we'd crawled our way to the top of the mound and peered down the other side, what we saw stopped us in our tracks. Tucked into the shrubs at the edge of the tree line, surrounded by a knee-high, wrought iron fence, was a cemetery. With the way the headstones leaned haphazardly in no specific order, it reminded me more of a burial ground. Jutting into the air in all directions, the markers looked like the oversized teeth you try to bust out with a baseball at the fair.

"Fuck me."

"Uhhhm," Garrett said, then giggled like a schoolgirl. He knew I usually didn't use that word. I don't know why. Neither of us was afraid to roll with vulgarities when we felt like it. We could spew profanity with the best sailors, truck drivers and reality show stars out there. But, for some reason, I always reserved that one word for the really special occasions, and if anything warranted it, it was stumbling upon an old, creepy graveyard in the middle of the creepy woods on one of the creepiest evenings I'd ever experienced. Especially a graveyard like this one, tossed together and, intentionally or not, hidden from the outside world. It just didn't feel right, and my insides reacted accordingly.

Against my silent wishes and everything he should've learned from the slasher films, Garrett made his way down the slope, slipping and sliding the whole way. He nearly busted his ass twice, and all I could do was watch from the top of the hill. I believe I have already mentioned Garrett's balls and their sheer size. As for me, I couldn't have been more frozen in place if the mud had sucked my shoes into the earth.

"Come on," he called back, but I didn't budge. I mean, I nearly pissed myself when I saw that first crooked headstone rising up out of the tall grass. The last thing I wanted to do was go exploring them closer.

"Do you really think we should?" I asked, as a stray gust of wind found me and sent a shiver down my already wet spine. "I mean, seriously."

From Garrett's own mouth came motivation.

"Pussy."

And there it was. Without even having to look back in my direction, Garrett knew just how to get me off that rise and down there beside him. Every guy knows that when your best friend throws down by calling you a pussy, you can't just give in and confirm it. You've gotta take the bait and turn it into an opportunity to prove him wrong. So with hesitation holding on to the back of my jacket, I sucked it up, slid sideways down the slope and joined him at the foot of the cemetery.

The short, wrought iron fence that surrounded the area was rusted and fallen over in several places. I nudged it with the toe of my muddy shoe and an entire section collapsed in on itself.

"This ain't keeping anything out," I said.

"Or anything in," Garrett added without hesitating, and that creeped me out even more. He always had that ability, to take things one step further. Especially when he knew he could get to me. It was fun for him and I was always party to it whether I wanted to be or not.

The scattered headstones were old. Most were small and flat, with nothing ornate about any of them as far as I could see. No large crosses or sculpted angels rose from the tops. No brass urns or modern photo plates were mounted on any of them. In fact, most were simple thin slabs of grey-white granite, leaning this way and that. The only thing on them was green and brown moss. If any had inscriptions chiseled into their façade, they'd worn smooth over time and were even more difficult to read in the near darkness that had fallen around us. Even when I pulled out my phone and used the backlight to illuminate the stones, it was only by running my fingers over the subtle contours and reading them like brail that I was barely able to make out a word or number here or there. The only full date I found that wasn't too rubbed out was November 13, 1921, but the face of that particular stone was in such disrepair, I couldn't even tell whether it was the date of birth or of death.

Somewhere in the sky outside the canopy of trees, lightning flashed again. In the moment of illumination that trickled through the trees, Garrett stepped around a large bush, then jumped back in shock.

"Fuck me!"

I heard the words just before the sonic crack of thunder filled the air like an omen. I knew it meant something bad. Garrett also hardly ever used that word.

Bone **10** White

One time, when Garrett and I were about twelve years old, we saw something that freaked us out big time, leaving an impression against which I would always measure everything else. It was late summer, and if you know anything about August in the Midwest, the heat can be oppressive. The humidity alone will suck the air right out of your lungs. So like a lot of kids who don't have a pool to cool off in, we spent the majority of our days shirtless and in cutoffs, wading through the streams that wound through and around New Paris. As we spent our last day of summer break exploring and chucking rocks in the shallow stream behind Mr. Nickerson's dairy farm, Garrett stumbled over a severed calf's head. I mean, literally tripped right over it and fell face first in the shallow water. It would have been funny, and I would have been more than happy to laugh my ass off if I hadn't already seen what caused him to trip. But I had. And that changed everything.

The head looked like it had been there awhile, all rotten and retched. The patchy white hair no longer white, but more the color of piss-stained sheets, flowed freely in the rippling water. Every few seconds, a stronger current would splash against it and momentarily shoo away angry flies. The eye sockets were hollow, and although it was too decomposed to tell for sure, the top of its skull looked like it had been bashed in.

The shock on Garrett's face that day, as he sat in ankle-deep water staring at the severed head at his feet, was one that I would never forget. Very nearly the same look I saw on his face now in the cemetery. Pale and bewildered. At a loss for words.

Garrett took another step back from the bush before looking fully in my direction. His mouth hung slack jawed, his eyes were wide.

"Luke."

It came out as little more than a whisper. I had barely even heard him say my name over the howling wind and rain, but I could still detect an unfamiliar quiver in his voice.

I circled around the bush and sludged warily through the mud to where Garrett stood with his eyes still fixed on something. I was already freaked out by the whole situation, and whatever had made Garrett's face go that pale threatened my very resolve before I had even seen what it was. My thoughts went to the missing girls. Part of me expected to find another severed head, and maybe not a calf's this time.

Then I saw it. What Garrett had seen. I saw it, and I stopped where I stood, frozen from the shock of not only the image, but the bizarre implications.

Laid out before us were three headstones just like all the others in the cemetery, crooked and covered with moss, their white granite worn and old. The names were barely an impression and no longer relevant to anyone living. What made these three different than the other markers, however, were the graves they were marking. Freshly churned soil rose above the rest of the ground in front of two of the headstones. Raw earth turning to mud. Rainwater trickling between the clumps. Despite the antique headstones, these two graves were new.

Beside them, a third grave.

An open one.

Marked by the third headstone, the edges of the casket-sized hole were crude and jagged. It was not a grave dug by a machine, its edges smooth and straight like the one I'd watched them lower my grandmother into a year ago.

This grave was dug by hand.

With a shovel.

Minutes later, my hands were shaking as we stood in the middle of the gravel driveway trying to decide what to do. I was wet and cold, and pretty sure my hands would have been shaking regardless, but Garrett was already looking around, appearing already recovered from the shock.

"We've gotta follow this driveway all the way to the house," Garrett argued, as he stood with his hands in his pockets, stomping mud off his shoes.

"Like hell, we do," I said, more abruptly than I'd meant to. "I say we go back to the road and keep walking until we find another house. Or, at least another creepy driveway."

"How do we even know the house and the graveyard are connected? How do we know –"

"It's on the same property, Garrett!" I exclaimed. "Beside the f'ing driveway!" I knew I was being short, but I couldn't help it. I felt like nothing good could come from proceeding to the house at the end of the driveway. Absolutely nothing. And besides that, I was scared. I admit it. By every possible definition, scared shitless.

"Okay. Calm down," Garrett urged, putting his hands out toward me as if that was going to do the trick. "You're probably right. Whoever owns the house probably owns the graveyard, too. But, how do we even know something's wrong here? Maybe there's a perfectly logical explanation for those graves being the way they are."

I looked at Garrett like that was the most ridiculous statement I had ever heard him make. And, quite frankly, it may very well have been.

"They're old graves," I said. "Almost a hundred years old, easily. And two of them have recently been dug up. By hand, I might add. And the third one is completely empty! Now how the hell can there be a logical explanation for that?"

We stood there for probably thirty more seconds as the trees around us swayed in the wind like arms at a hip-hop concert. Garrett had nothing. No reasonable argument to make. Occasionally I was right about things and this was possibly one of those times. Probably was, in fact. But, there was still that something in Garrett's eyes. That something that told me I should trust his judgment. I'd seen it before, and to his credit, he had never steered me wrong. Still, I fought the voice in my head telling me to give in.

I tried to zip my jacket up to stall for time, but the zipper was already maxed out against my chin. I was shivering. From the rain and wind? Or from what I had seen at the cemetery? Who knows? Just the same, my resignation was wavering, and I wasn't happy about it.

"Luke. Dude," Garrett started, then took a long look in the direction of the house that wasn't yet visible, hidden somewhere among trees that were more menacing than they had been only minutes before. He turned back to me for a second, then cast his eyes back toward the main road, procrastinating, choosing his words carefully. Making sure that whatever he said to me would get the result he wanted.

"I really don't wanna walk for who knows how much longer before we find another house," he said like he regretted the decision so I would agree with him. "It could be miles, Luke. And in this weather, that means hours."

As if he somehow planned it, Mother Nature gave him a hand just then with another rumble of thunder echoing somewhere beyond the trees. The sound of rain spattering the treetops intensified, and the temperature dropped as I stood there. The fear was holding fast, but the fight was draining out of me with the stream of water running off my nose.

My shoulders sagged with defeat and, uttering that word I rarely said, I walked past Garrett down a long driveway toward a house that may or may not have a good explanation for the empty grave in its abandoned cemetery.

PART II

You are of your father the devil,
and your will is to do your father's desires.
- John 8:44

Bone **11** White

She rolled the severed finger across the floor like a marble. Like a toy car. Its sinewy flesh was already drying, already shrinking away from the exposed bone protruding from one end. With every push, the finger bumped and tumbled across the uneven wood planks.

She had long stopped caring for the girls. No longer felt sorry for them. She had shed tears over the first girl, but Father had corrected her. Rightfully so. We don't cry over them. They're just objects. Sometimes playthings when time allowed. But, nothing to cry over either way. Nothing at all.

Picking up the severed finger, she laid it on top of her own. Even in its deteriorating condition, she thought the other girl's was prettier. She liked the pink painted nail, even though some of the polish had chipped during the struggle. It reminded her of bubblegum, that long forgotten novelty. Even the wrinkled skin, she could tell, had been beautiful and unblemished, not filthy and scarred like her own. She could feel the envy rising up and had to steel herself against its familiar pull. Squash it.

Stupid girl. Her father's voice.

Scowling, she turned the finger over and looked at the end, at the bone itself, sticking out just slightly. She wondered what the inside of her own finger looked like. Were her bones as beautiful and white as this one? Could they bring money, also? Or, more likely, was the inside of her body just as tainted, just as wretched and cruel looking as the outside? She imagined it was, but still wondered. Maybe someday she'd find out. Just cut off one of her own fingers. Maybe a toe. Did she need them all? Certainly not. Someday. Maybe someday she'd do it.

Her father's footsteps thumped on the stairs. She slid the finger into her dress pocket and made a mental note to return it to his workbench so he wouldn't notice it was missing among the arms, legs and feet. And hands. Those delicate hands. It was her father's work. And he was so busy lately.

Bone **12** White

The house turned out not to be a house at all, but rather a small church. Abandoned. The long, winding drive with its once prestigious-looking gate posts lured me to expect a grand estate lingering at the end. Lord knows there were a few of them scattered around the lake. Garrett and I were always gawking at them from the boat as we fished. Two and three-story monoliths made of glass and stone with their paver walkways leading down to boat houses with televisions and fully stocked bars. I always wondered what these people did for a living to be able to afford such luxury.

No such wealth waited at the end of this driveway, though. The dilapidated building had probably been painted white, like many of the small churches you see on television and scattered along country roads. Quaint, is how my mother would have described it. But, this church's best days were behind it, and the clapboard siding was now gray and weathered. That much was obvious even in the limited light. Dark spots, probably moss, lounged on the siding like uninvited guests overstaying their welcome. Black shutters, at least the ones that still remained, hung by a single nail or two, crooked and abstract, straddling long, boarded up windows. Even some of those boards hung precariously by only a nail or two. And towering over the entire dilapidated structure was the large pointed spire, rising up above the awning that sheltered the double doors of the entrance.

The tiny churchyard, surrounded by the fortress walls of the dense woods, wasn't faring much better. No one had cut the grass in years and it had largely succumbed to an invasion of dandelions. Long forgotten shrubs, creeping well beyond their sunken-bricked borders, were all that passed as landscaping. Lining the front and side of the church, their hundreds of tiny finger-like branches shot out in every direction, shaking in the wind as if to warn people away.

A tin-roofed shed sat behind the main building, up against the foreboding woods. The tiny structure leaned to one side so much, the wind and rain threatened to bring it down at any minute. That would be doing it a favor. Put it out of its misery. But then, looking at it from my point of view, the same could have been said about the church itself.

The only purpose the dismal shed still served was bearing a floodlight that rose a few feet above the metal roof. The weak light's glow barely reached the ground. At first, it gave me hope that someone would be here, but looking at it again, I realized it was the type of light that could be set to come on at dark, then shut off when daylight approached. It had probably been turning itself on and off for years, like a lonely lighthouse keeper who remains on the job long after the shipping channels had been rerouted.

We stood at the edge of the canopy of trees, where the driveway gave itself up to the parking lot. No longer protected, the rain was coming down on us like we were standing under an industrial-sized showerhead. I would have given anything at that moment for an umbrella. Even one of my mother's colorful umbrellas with the flowers and butterflies on it. Hell, it would have brightened up the place. And maybe my mood.

"Now what?" I shouted to Garrett, competing with a rumble of thunder from overhead.

He just shrugged.

"Well, maybe there's no phone, but there's definitely shelter from all this," he said, holding his arms out to indicate everything that was coming down on us. The rain. Thunder. Lightning. Wind. Darkness.

All of it.

Then, with a punch to my arm, he left me standing there by myself. Creating tiny explosions of water with every step, he sprinted across the overgrown yard and up the concrete steps leading underneath the smallest of overhangs. I watched him cup his hand around his eyes to look through a large cross-shaped window in one of the doors, his shoulders scrunched up to keep his ears warm. The scene reminded me of many I'd seen on television late at night. After midnight, the only things worth watching were low budget horror films and infomercials. In those films, young people were always doing things they shouldn't be, only to end up in black body bags with shiny silver zippers. In the infomercials, beautiful women with perfect hair and professionally done nails tried to sell us products we really didn't need, but were guaranteed to make our lives easier. They usually threw in a second, vaguely related item, offering you both for the incredible low price of $19.95. I'd never been sure which program was scarier, but scanning the scene of decay and neglect before me, I didn't see any other young people or beautiful women. But then, I didn't have a credit card anyway.

"Shit," I mumbled, and started across the parking lot.

Bone **13** White

Running up the steps to the stoop, I was immediately aware of two things: the first was that the church had a sorrowful air, like nothing good had happened here for a long, long time. The second was that I regretted being aware of the first. The last thing I needed was to walk into a freakin' sorrowful church.

Garrett was still peering through stained glass emblazoned with deep shades of red, yellow, purple and blue. By the looks of his expression, he wasn't seeing anything promising inside. As dark as it was, I would have been surprised if he'd been able to see much of anything, especially with nearly all the church's windows boarded up.

Having been raised right, I'd worried about tracking mud on someone's floors when we decided to head this way, but looking at this place, the worry disappeared. At least *that* worry. There were plenty more to replace it. But, if the inside of the church was anything like the outside, tracks of mud would go unnoticed. And there was no reason to believe the inside had fared any better.

"Anyone home?" I asked, knowing full well there wasn't.

Garrett shook his head.

"Nah. Guess they're not handing out candy this year."

He smiled, but I wasn't in the mood. Not with my entire body shivering and my teeth chattering like a wind-up toy. He must have taken the hint, because the grin faded.

"Can't even see much, really," Garrett continued. "Looks like there's something covering the window on the door."

"Could be too dark," I offered.

"I don't think so," he said. "I should at least be able to see something. But, it's like there's not even a window there. Might as well be trying to look through the wall."

Before I could say anything, Garrett had his hand on the scrolled iron door handle and was pushing down on the button. Nothing happened, so he jiggled it harder, the next step on the universally known list of things to do when you encounter a locked door. Still nothing.

"Locked."

"Good," I said and meant it. With all my heart. We were out of the rain, and the thought of heading back into it wasn't exactly appealing, but this place was creeping me out more with every minute we spent here, especially with the image of the empty grave still fresh in my mind. All I wanted to do was put some distance between us and this entire property, storm or not. "Guess we should move on," I suggested. "We can't get in, and there's obviously no one here."

Garrett was too busy checking out the cross-shaped window on the other door to respond. I'm not sure he even heard me over the rain hitting the roof of the awning like the steel wheels of a train click-clacking over the seams in the rails. I thought about repeating myself, then quickly forgot all about it when some gold lettering caught my eye. The words were painted on a dark, wooden board mounted beside the church's entrance doors. Getting right up on it, I could make out the words "Register of Attendance and Offering" across the top. Down the left hand side was a list of words in the same gold, only this lettering was smaller and more difficult to read. Even so, it only took a moment to realize what it was. The board told the church members how many people had attended services this week versus last week. It also told them the amount of offering collected the present week versus the last. Basically, it was a holy scoreboard.

"Interesting," I muttered, looking over at Garrett to see if he had noticed the board. He hadn't. He was still focused on the windows, so I turned my attention back to the board. Three of the four slots were empty. No info there. One slot, however, the one that said "Attendance Today," had a lone wooden tile in its slot. A number two in the same gold lettering. At first, I wondered if it was a joke. *Two? Really?* Then I started to wonder if things had really gotten that bad in the end.

"Same thing here," Garrett said. "Nothing but black. This window seems like it's actually covered up from the inside. Maybe painted over."

"Shit," I said, forgetting the attendance board and jamming my cold hands deeper into my shorts pockets. I was on the hunt for a heat source and was having little luck finding it. "Why would someone do that? I mean, from the looks of it, it's not like this church has any treasure to hide."

"Yeah," Garrett said, with the first hint of uncertainty in his voice. He wasn't feeling as comfortable with the decision to come here as he once was.

The fact that someone had taken the trouble to cover the windows on the inside of a church as remote as this one might have been a huge red flag for most people. A sign that we weren't wanted here. For me, though, it was just one of many small red flags I had already seen. They'd been popping up left and right over the past hour, each one adding to the unease growing in the pit of my stomach. But then, really, how much more screwed up could this little fishing trip get?

The moment the question entered my mind, I was already regretting it. I should have known better. One, because levels of "screwed up" are always subjective. And two, because every question has an answer.

I turned my back to the church, stood at the edge of the steps and looked out among the trees. Only twenty feet of unkempt yard separated the trees on the front from the entrance to the church. The building sat on a slight hill, so the rain ran in narrow rivers through the saturated yard toward the patch of woods between the church and the lake. If I rose on my tiptoes, and strained my neck just enough, I could see a thin stretch of the water. On the other side of the lake, a street lamp shimmered on its surface. It was probably only a few miles away, though it might as well be on the other side of the Earth.

A gust of wind blew across the stoop, rattling a board that was loosely covering a front window and causing me to draw my arms in closer. My collar was already turned up and my hands were as deep in my pockets as they could go. I was still freezing, and my heart grew heavy as I realized this was probably as warm as I was going to get for a while.

"What now, Captain?" I asked.

When Garrett gave no answer, I turned around to offer my own suggestion, but there was no one there to listen.

Bone **14** White

Most of the dolls still had their heads, but not all of them. Some didn't even have arms or legs anymore. But, at least their torsos allowed them to sit upright in the chairs and that was all she needed. She was too old to play with dolls, too old by nearly a decade. Yet, Father had insisted on turning the tiny room into a makeshift classroom, trying to make up for the fact that she didn't have any friends, and she couldn't disappoint him. He had even hung an old cracked blackboard on one of the walls. The six tiny chairs he'd found in the basement when they'd first moved in were the perfect size for the dolls to sit in and listen as she taught them all the things she remembered from school.

It wasn't a lot.

Above all else, she made sure to teach them the number one rule. Not the Golden Rule, but her father's rule. Stressed it every chance she got, just like he had done with her. The students would learn it, even if it killed them. Learn it and live by it, just like she did.

Outside, the storm raged and rattled the walls. And as the evening wore on, she found herself spending more time soothing the fears of her dolls and less time on their lessons. Especially Hannah. Hannah was always the most scared. And she was a screamer. Screamed more than the others. Way more. Hannah's high pitched shrieks still echoed in her ears.

Storms didn't really bother her, though. Very little scared her anymore. Her father was a master of death, so what was there to fear? And he was such a good father. This one loved her, she was sure. He told her so, over and over. He showed her. He would never leave her, not like the other one. She would make sure of it. She would be so good.

Bone 15 White

"Shit."

I saw no sign of Garrett anywhere on the church grounds. How had he vanished so fast? He had to be nearby. As I took one last glimpse at the attendance board and hopped down the steps, the rain ratcheted up a notch. For some reason, that lone number two tile bugged me. It could be that all the other tiles had blown away over time or been stolen by vandals. I wasn't sure what anyone would want with wooden number tiles, but it was a more comforting thought than there truly only being two people left at the congregation's end.

With the rain coming down harder than it had before, I slopped my way through the swampy grass toward the side yard. Before I'd gotten far, something caught my eye, something I hadn't seen when I ran up to the steps, shielding my face from the rain. Tucked behind an overambitious shrub stood an old wooden sign, its white paint more chipped and missing than not. With rainwater running into my eyes, I drew aside the branches, revealing the words carved into the wood.

New Congregational Church

Sunday School............9:00 am
A.M. Worship............10:30 am
P.M. Worship............7:00 pm
Thursday Worship........7:00 pm

Visitors Welcome
Est. 1927.

As wet and cold as I was, a chill still managed to run down my back, and an uneasy feeling came over me. Something about the sign made things more personal. The church's demise, more sorrowful. I stepped back and the shrub once again covered the sign. I tried to laugh off my nerves as I continued to the side of the building. *Visitors welcome.* Yeah right. I didn't feel welcome here at all.

I cleared the corner, expecting to see Garrett peering into one of the side windows. But, there was no sign of him.

Damn it!

Saying I was getting nervous would be a bigger understatement than saying all this rain was going to make mud. I wasn't finding myself thrilled about being there, period, much less alone. Somewhere in my head I knew Garrett must have just gone the other way around the building, but it didn't stop a slight degree of fear from setting in. My nerves were on edge, pulled as taut as piano wire, and the slap of the rain on the mud was about to make them snap.

I was just about to head back to the front stoop and hang out like a lost child hoping for his parent's return, when something moved near the back corner of the church, a darker blotch against its already dark surroundings. It looked like a person, probably Garrett, but I couldn't be certain. And that bothered me even more.

"Garrett," I whispered, and felt my face flush in the cold wind. *Idiot.* No one was going to hear me over the wind and pounding rain. And maybe it was better they hadn't heard me. For all I knew, it wasn't Garrett at all, but a deranged lunatic who liked to dig up graves and wear the rotting skin as a mask. Cue my mother's speech about horror movies. "You watch too many of those things. They give you nightmares. Blah, blah, blah."

The dark form turned, hesitating for a moment, before trudging through the tall, wet grass in my direction. My stomach came up into my chest, pushing my heart into my throat. Eighteen different options rushed into my mind, things I could do, actions I could take, but I didn't move on any of them. More out of fear than bravery, I stood my ground. My feet simply weren't listening to what my head was telling them. I wasn't even sure the message was getting through. All I found myself able to do was shield my eyes against the stinging rain, and attempt to get a better look at the person. Bad idea. I got a better look, but didn't like what I saw. Whoever it was, they were carrying something in one of their hands. Something Garrett hadn't had. Something long. Something thin. A machete? Axe?

With every possibility that entered my mind, more wet hairs stood on the back of my neck. I took an involuntary step back, then two. Instinctively, my hands came out of my pockets, but I wasn't sure why. I wasn't much of a fighter. I was just about to turn and run when a flash of lightning lit up everything within several square miles.

And I saw the familiar red jacket.

Garrett was coming toward me carrying a length of 2x4. Relief flooded my chest and allowed some of the tension stored up in my body to ease. I realized that I'd been holding my breath, so I let it out. My shoulders relaxed and the tight crease that stretched across my forehead dissolved with the rain. Garrett and I had been friends since the first grade, and I can't remember when I'd ever been happier to see that kid.

"Hey," Garrett said when he finally drew within an audible distance.

"Hey, yourself," I reproached, jamming my hands back into the semi-warmth of my shorts pockets. "Don't ever do that again." Then, before he could ask, "Disappear on me like that."

"Sorry, man, but we weren't getting anywhere just standing around with our hands in our pockets."

Trying to draw as little attention as I could, I slowly pulled my hands from my shorts.

"What's the board for?" I asked, deciding not to make too big of a deal about him leaving me behind. Knowing me the way he did, Garrett probably knew I was getting spooked. No reason to prove it to him.

He shrugged, holding up the piece of wood so I could get a better look at it.

"Two by four," he said, smacking the wood against an open palm. "Just in case."

And it was then that I knew I wasn't the only one scared. Standing out here in the dark and stormy night beside an abandoned church with, let's be honest, some pretty disturbing elements to it, Garrett was getting just as freaked out as I was. And the very idea of that both relieved and frightened me.

"Man, I'm freezin' my cherries off here," I said, hoping to capitalize on my friend's newfound misgivings. "Let's move on down the road."

"Don't have to," he said, with a nod toward the rear of the church. "Back door's unlocked."

Despite the near darkness, he must have seen the look on my face because he started coaxing.

"Dude, it's dry inside. We can finally get out of this shit and warm up."

I opened my mouth to argue, but something stopped the words dead. A sound. A loud shrieking sound, almost like a scream. With the wind swirling around us, I couldn't pinpoint the direction the anguished sound had come from. The woods? Inside the church? I couldn't even tell what kind of creature had made the sound, but the hairs rose further on my neck.

Garrett and I caught each other's eyes in the dim light. It was a relief knowing I wasn't just hearing things, but that relief was tainted with the sour taste of fear. Garrett's eyes were wide.

"The fuck was that?"

Bone 16 White

We eased the door shut ever so gently. I wasn't exactly sure why. I doubted anyone was within earshot of this place, nor would a subtle creak from an old back door be heard over what was going on outside anyway. The storm was full on and this old clapboard church had very little defense against the tempest. The fierce wind was playing it like a musical instrument, and any sound the door might make would have been one among thousands. Still, being cautious just seemed like the right protocol for a situation that might just call for it.

As for the shriek, neither of us was sure where it had come from. No clue. The woods was our best guess, so we'd decided not to spend any more time outside when we could be doing our contemplating where it was dry and warm. Though I use the word "warm" in a completely relative manner, because the room we were in was anything but.

We were standing in what my grandmother would have called a mudroom. She'd had one that separated her kitchen from her garage and used it for storage more than anything. Jars of beans and preserves and anything else that required storage in a cool dry place lined the shelves around the room. Her aprons, boots, gloves, tools and anything else she used to work in the garden just outside the door was kept there as well. As for why she called it a mudroom, it probably had to do with the fact that if we entered the house without leaving our dirty shoes on the mat inside the door, well then, she would let us know about it. And believe me, she may be as sweet an old lady as you'd ever meet, but you didn't want to "hear about it" from my grandmother.

This room wasn't as welcoming as my grandmother's. The smell was the first difference. The tiny room lacked the natural mustiness and old wood smell of my grandmother's mudroom, but instead, the not-so-subtle odor of iron, earth and oil permeated the air. And bleach. The scent of bleach alone hovered in the room like a lost cloud. The close confines of the windowless space made it worse. There was nowhere for the caustic air to go, and the odor was so strong that I wondered how we hadn't smelled it even from outside.

I gagged just a bit, and Garrett put his hand on my arm. I fought back another reflux, took a slow breath of air through my nose and nodded to my friend that I was alright. Or, at least I nodded to where I thought he was. With the door closed, it was difficult to see much else in the pitch black room.

"Cellphone," Garrett whispered, and once again I nodded.

Together, Garrett and I flipped our phones open. The intent was to use them for light, but that didn't stop me from checking mine for service. The screen showed one bar for a moment and my eyes perked up. But, before my thumb could hit the button with the outline of a phone on it, the bar was gone again, replaced with a tiny white X. I was once again in a dead spot and, after holding the phone up at different angles with the same result, my focus returned to shedding some light on our situation.

We held our cells out before us like cops displaying badges, and the first thing we spotted was a tilted and wobbly looking washer and dryer unit positioned against one wall. Why the hell was there a washer and dryer sitting in an abandoned church? I mean, they fit the décor—old and rickety—like I expected everything else in this building to be. But, the sheer fact that they were even here seemed strange to me. Both were covered in a dark substance that could have been either rust or mud or something else altogether. Garrett motioned for me to lift the lid on the washer, and I told him what I thought of the idea with my middle finger. His blue-shaded alien face broke into a grin, and it was comforting to see.

I turned away from Garrett in the efforts of revealing more interesting things in the room. Actually, it was mostly to discourage any more of his suggestions. The soft blue light illuminated a room that was barely large enough for two people to move around in. In the corner beside the washer and dryer sat a bucket. The long wooden handle of a stringy mop stuck out and rested against the wall. Oddly, in contrast to the appliances beside it, the bright red bucket looked relatively new. The sticker on the side looked to be just as fresh as the day it was put on at the factory.

A narrow shelf clung to the wall just above the washer, supporting an assortment of small plastic bottles, their faded labels fuzzy from the thin layer of dust on them. Beside the old bottles sat a cleaner one, a fat white bottle with the familiar blue and red Clorox label stretched across its belly. Resting on the shelf beside it was a small blue cap, and I understood then why the room smelled as it did. My first impulse was to reach up and put the cap back on the bottle, but then I decided against it. The imprisoned air was already thick with the smell of bleach, and I wasn't planning on sticking around much longer anyway. Besides, I felt like a child being towed into a store full of fine china and glassware. The voice in my head took on a parental tone.

Don't touch anything!

Leaving the cap where it sat, I moved beyond the dryer, washer and the shelf above it, to where things got real interesting. Back toward the door we'd just entered sat a couple of pairs of old boots, piled in a heap. Old mud clung to the soles in dry, cracked clumps. The evidence of another person's belongings in the church was enough to send a shiver up my spine, but what we saw next beat that all to hell. Just above the boots, on a crooked and rusty nail, hung a raincoat. A wet and muddy raincoat. Dripping. Glistening.

I almost pissed my pants.

Garrett and I exchanged looks that said we'd both noticed the same thing. Part of me had hoped that my eyes were playing tricks on me in the dim light, but Garrett had seen the raindrops on the coat as well. My heart started beating overtime, and I gasped when the light from my phone went black. In the instant before I could turn my phone back on, the weak light from Garrett's phone illuminated something else we hadn't noticed. I pushed the button to refresh the backlight on my phone and swept it around to where Garrett's had just been. Cast in a shadowy blue haze were two wooden steps leading up to what must have been the entry door to the main part of the church. Tall and imposing from my vantage point two steps below, the wooden door looked like it guarded the entrance to somewhere far more menacing than an abandoned church out in the country.

A thin sliver of dim light eked from beneath the door, illuminating nothing. In fact, it barely shone brighter than the rest of the murky area, but, if you looked close, it was definitely a light, and thoughts of the raincoat came rushing back.

Dripping wet. Glistening.

"Shit! We're not alone," I hissed, shutting my cell phone down, as the thumping inside my chest became deafening. Without moving my eyes from the dim strip of light, I blindly reached behind me to Garrett's damp jacket. I gave it a couple tugs, and after some shuffling of feet, I could feel him beside me.

"What'd you say?" he asked.

"Check it out," I whispered, although my voice was an octave higher making is sound more like a squeak. "The light. The raincoat. Someone's actually here!" With its dark windows, the thought that someone might be in the church had never even crossed our minds. At least I know it hadn't mine, and I was pretty sure Garrett would have mentioned it had it crossed his. But, the signs were quickly stacking up in the favor of us not being alone in the church.

"Maybe," Garrett replied. "Think we can get the door open without making any sound?"

"What!?!" I exclaimed, in a combination gasp and whisper. "You've seen this place. All old and creaky and shit. If there's even a possibility that someone is here, we should back out now and knock on the front door. We didn't even think of that, did we?"

I would have described the look on Garrett's face as skeptical, if not doubtful. But, then, as distorted as his face looked in the haunting light of his cell phone, any emotion or expression was possible.

"Is that really what you want to do?" he asked. "Go back out in the rain and knock on the front door?"

"No," I said in a more hushed voice than I was feeling. "What I really want to do is go back to the fuckin' boat, motor my ass back to the truck and drive it back home so I can get out of these fuckin' wet clothes and get warm!" I closed my eyes and started rubbing my temple at my outburst. I was freaking out over the entire situation, and that wasn't doing either of us any good.

Garrett gave me a moment before speaking up.

"Are you finished?"

Without opening my eyes, I continued rubbing my temples and nodded.

"Okay," he said. "I just wanna take a peek. The light's not very bright, so I doubt it means anyone's nearby. Who knows? Maybe it's one of those security lights that comes on automatically, like the one on the shed. Maybe it's just a light from an exit sign over the door."

"And the raincoat?"

"I don't know. Maybe somebody lives here."

"Yeah, like a vampire maybe," I said. I regretted it the moment the words left my mouth. No, earlier. The moment the image formed in my head, once I'd seen the way all the windows were covered. Even though I knew what was coming, my skin still crawled.

"Vampires?" Garrett asked. "Really?" He shook his head slowly. "Your mom might be right about you taking a break from the horror flicks. Nothing more than PG stuff for you. Gonna have to stick to Disney."

"Stuff it," I said in my defense. "I don't mean like real vampires. But maybe some twisted guy who thinks he's a vampire, or even just a hermit who doesn't fancy intruders. And what are we doing? Intruding."

"Okay. I'll give you that everything about this place spells weird. But I want to know what its story is."

Like every decision since the boat broke down, I was pretty sure this, too, was a bad idea. But, Garrett was the one in control. It was his boat and his idea to come on this excursion, so by default, this was his command. And as freaked out and afraid as I was, that meant his judgment was more trustworthy.

He was a good leader, a better friend, and he'd never steered me wrong. Besides, if he was truly set on checking out the rest of the church, the last thing I was going to do was walk away and leave my friend behind.

"New Congregational Church," I said, after a quiet moment. "What religion does that sound like to you?"

"What?" Garrett asked, the shadows on his face taking on a quizzical nature.

"The sign. Out front. It says New Congregational Church on it. Just wondering what religion that might be."

"Does it really matter?" Garrett asked.

I let my shrug answer for me. It didn't really matter; it was just a stall tactic on my part.

Garrett reached for the knob as I backed him up with the light from my cell. With my heart in my stomach, I watched his hand close around the knob and marveled at the fact that it wasn't shaking. Mine were. The light from my phone was shimmering on the walls like a strobe in a dance club. And I couldn't quite remember how to breathe.

The knob turned in his hand and a faint click was heard as the latch disengaged. My pulse kicked into high gear as Garrett calmly turned and looked at me, a wry grin on his pale blue face.

"So, when was the last time you played Rip the Drapes?"

And that was when my internal warning system went through the roof, sirens blaring, as my eyes reacted to the implications of what he was asking. They had to have been the size of Ping-Pong balls. They had to have been full of alarm.

Bone **17** White

She'd had enough. The students were being unruly and uncooperative, and she was done with them. They were talking when they should have been listening, answering questions without raising their hands and giggling when someone would give the wrong answer. All the things they knew better than to do. They knew how things were supposed to work in her classroom. They'd been doing this a long time now.

So they were sitting in silence with their heads down, being punished, while she retreated upstairs to her side of the bedroom she shared with her father. The students would be lucky if she even returned this evening. She didn't think she would. Maybe in the morning. *Make 'em suffer.*

She used the rickety wooden handrail on the stairs, even though she could easily do it without its help. She'd probably gone up and down these stairs a thousand times in the dark. Maybe even a hundred thousand. Father didn't like using the lights, and rarely did, even though they still worked. Didn't like using candles even, allowing their use only in times of necessity. Or sometimes when she was playing school, but he preferred her do that during the day. At first he'd said no this night, but the thunder and lightning had chipped away his resolve. No one would be out in this weather to see the light. And he knew the students' company comforted her while he did his work. The students might be dolls, but they played a bigger role when the loneliness became unbearable.

She jumped over the last step at the top of the stairs, not because she was worried someone would hear the creak that it made, but because the shrill sound was like fingernails on a chalkboard to her ears. It was a high-pitched, slow emanation of sound that she couldn't stand, so she always tried to remember to hop up onto the second floor landing without waking the monster. Especially when she was taking the stairs at night and all around her was dark.

Inside the room, she crawled across her father's bed, nothing but a stained mattress thrown onto the floor, and set her feet down on the worn wood on the other side. The loft itself was tiny, and the old mattress stretched from one end to the other. Crawling across it was the only way to reach her bed.

Searching the darkness, her thin fingers fell upon the dingy sheet that served as a curtain, separating the two sides of the room. She pulled the rough linen along the rope until it stopped, taking care not to pull the hook out of the wall again. Father hadn't been happy with her carelessness last time and had let her know about it. She'd learned the lesson and had been extra careful ever since.

She stretched out on her bed, just another mattress on the floor, and let the darkness consume her. The students had given her a headache, and she was happy to be alone. Her father was off somewhere and the curtain was hardly needed. Still, the sheer piece of cloth made her feel like she had her own room again. A place she could retreat to when she wanted, at least for awhile. Soon enough, Father would be done with his work for the night and would come upstairs looking for her. Soon enough, she would no longer be alone. Soon enough.

Bone **18** White

When Garrett and I were kids, we used to turn off all the lights at night and take turns ripping open the drapes and pressing our faces against the windowpane. There was just something about the nighttime on the other side of the glass that made it scary. The unknown, and what could be out there lurking around. It was supposed to be a fear factor type thing to see which of us already had balls at that age. But it usually only resulted in giggles and boasts of yet untested bravery. I'll never forget, though, the night with my cousins at my aunt's big, old house on the edge of town. Similar to the church, her house was surrounded on two sides by thick clumps of evergreens. Behind the house was nothing but a patch of woods that went for almost a half mile. Figuring we were in a secluded enough area, my cousins and I played the game without fear, all of us fairly confident in the odds.

That confidence, however, proved short lived.

Everyone else had already taken a turn without incident when I finally got my chance. But when I threw open the drapes, someone was in the backyard. Dressed all in dark clothing, everything but the man's face was cloaked in black, blending into the night. His white eyes stared at me, watching as I stumbled backward so fast that I fell over my youngest cousin and we ended up in a heap. I scrambled to my feet and flung the drapes shut as quickly as I'd opened them, my young heart having just aged probably ten years.

We never found out who the man was, or what he was doing out there. With the game at an abrupt end, we spent the rest of the evening huddled on the couch, calming our nerves by telling ourselves it had just been our Uncle Joe sneaking a smoke. That explanation worked for some of us, even though others swore they'd heard Joe's voice in the kitchen at the time of the ripping.

Whoever it was, life went on and I got over it without any trips to a shrink or developing a bedwetting issue. But, standing in the church's back room, not knowing what was on the other side of this door, I was pretty sure that if Garrett ripped open that door like we used to the drapes, the panic alone would put me on a psychiatrist's couch for years.

Thankfully, he didn't do it. Instead, he eased the door open slowly. Maybe he thought that ripping it open would have been too much for me to handle, as if he knew what I'd been thinking. Or, just maybe, he wasn't as confident as his cockiness let on.

The softest ray of light crept into the mudroom as the door inched inward. It was immediately obvious that the light wasn't coming from the main room. It was too faint, not even bright enough for us to see clearly. But, it was enough that we could at least make out our surroundings, and allow us to snap our cellphones closed. Through the doorway, a section of the cavernous sanctuary revealed its shadowy expanse. We could just make out a few rows of pews closest to us. We each took a deep breath and exchanged hopeful looks, before cautiously climbing the two steps up into the room. Garrett in front, then me.

The light looked to be coming from a small room directly across the sanctuary from us. I couldn't see far into the lit room, but there was no movement, there were no sounds other than the wind howling outside, the rain hitting the roof and the moaning of the church in response to it all. But, there was definitely a light coming from the room.

Judging by the building's lack of size, the sanctuary itself was larger than I expected from the outside. Maybe the shadows stretching out from the lit room on the other side just made it look that way. Who knows? We hesitated just beyond the doorway, unsure what to do now that we were inside, and for the most part, unable to enjoy the fact that we were out of the rain. We stood there, taking it all in.

One of the first things I noticed were the long strips of heavy, black cloth that hung on the light colored walls every six or seven feet. Just about the same distance as the locations of the windows. Another strip, not nearly as long, but just as wide, hung in the middle of each of the doors at the entrance. Garrett must have noticed them about the same time, because we looked at each other with a nod of understanding. The strips of cloth were the reason we hadn't been able to see in the windows.

The makeshift drapes intrigued me enough that I put aside my fear and followed Garrett as he took a couple of steps farther into the room. I couldn't speak for him but I, for one, was enthralled. I'd never been inside, much less explored, an abandoned building. If I weren't shivering in my clinging wet clothes, I would have found the whole thing very cool. Maybe Garrett felt the same, because he kept going, with me right beside him. We were still cautious, but now more curious than anything else.

Rows of wooden pews with their deep purple cloth either ripped or eaten by mice took up the majority of the sanctuary. We passed a lonely black organ, covered in cobwebs and a thick layer of dust. A wooden and equally neglected bench rested beside the organ. One of its legs was broken and angled inward, causing the bench to lean awkwardly to the side. I half expected the organ to start playing by itself, like in some Bela Lugosi classic. Vampire movies came to mind, sending a chill down my spine. Thankfully, the organ hadn't seen any of those movies. It didn't know its designated role.

We made our way toward the back of the room, all the while keeping one eye on the lit side room and another on the floor where we were walking. We tiptoed to keep from making noise, but it was proving difficult. The floor between the pews was littered with papers and disheveled hymnals, scraps of a once thriving house of worship. The condition gave an atmosphere of chaos, like everyone had thrown the books and papers into the air, like graduates and their tasseled caps. Or maybe the house of worship had come under attack by Satanists intent on trashing the place, leaving no word of God unturned. I wiped my temple, sweating despite how cold I was. Maybe my mom was right. I needed to stop with the B-movies, already.

Turning to gauge Garrett's impression of the mess, my lungs and cardiac muscle jerked me back. From where we'd entered, we hadn't yet seen the altar, that front part of the church where the minister usually stands. Because if we had, we would have turned and high-tailed it out. Immediately.

Bone 19 White

A weathered wooden coffin played the role of the elephant in the room. Dirty and looking very old in its design, it perched upon the raised stage like an altar awaiting its sacrifice. A knee-high spindled railing surrounded the platform, a warning keeping us at bay, as if we needed to be told to be wary. With the shadows doing their best to conceal it all, I couldn't have overstated the chilling scene before us if I'd tried.

The shock of seeing the coffin must have been playing across my face, because Garrett's expression changed when our eyes finally met. His eyes narrowed, and his head cocked to one side.

"Luke?"

He hadn't seen the coffin, yet.

"Dude," I stammered, "check it out." I nodded in the direction of the closed coffin. Then, as if being pulled by some giant magnet, I started walking toward the death box before Garrett could even turn and look. My feet moved—left, right, left, right—one at a time without taking my eyes off the elongated wooden box. I couldn't. I was afraid if I looked away for even a second, it would be gone once I turned back, like a mirage or a ghost. I was a marionette with someone else working the strings. I just kept walking. I passed the rows of crumbling pews, weaving through the scattered hymnals here, kicking right through them there, until I stood at the foot of the raised pulpit. The break in the front railing served as an open invitation to anyone brave enough to come this far.

As I considered the weight of my intestinal fortitude, a sound came from above. A loud groan emanating from old wooden planks. I instinctively crouched down on one knee. Garrett's warm breath brushed across my neck, telling me that he had hit his knee, too. I made a gradual turn on my heels so that only he would hear my whisper.

"The wind?" I asked, eyebrows raised optimistically.

Garrett just shrugged. "Hope so."

We both raised our gaze toward the high ceiling that might as well have not even been there. Shadowy blackness was all we could see. There was no telling what laid beyond. I'd seen a tiny window from the outside, high enough to be from a second story. Maybe an attic, or loft of some kind, but I wasn't sure.

"I saw a stairway leading upstairs," Garrett whispered, as if reading my mind. "Back there. Off to the side. But, I don't think the sound came from upstairs. Sounded more like the wind playing havoc with the roof shingles to me."

"Maybe, but it seems pretty obvious that someone else is here," I whispered, although the words half stuck in my throat.

"And I'd say they have about as much right to be here as we do."

"And what about that?" I asked, pointing at the coffin.

"There's got to be some reasonable explanation," he said, but a slight hesitation told me he was acting more confident than he felt. He licked his dry lips in the dim light. "Fine. We'll save the upstairs for later," he said, making clear the concession was only temporary.

I gave Garrett a thumbs up and returned my attention to the coffin. Despite the opening in the railing, inviting us closer, where we stood was close enough for me. The force that had pulled me this far had ceased, like someone had grabbed ahold of my jacket from behind. But, it wasn't just the will to get closer that had deserted me. I no longer wanted to investigate the coffin period. For that matter, the church itself. Maybe I was afraid of what I would find. Maybe I was afraid of the knowledge I would have afterward. There are instances in life when it's just better not knowing. And for me, this was one of those times.

"I've seen enough," I whispered. "I can live the rest of my life not knowing what's in there." Turning and looking at his face in the near darkness, I struggled to read Garrett's expression. Was he feeling the same ominous sense that I was? Was he finally ready to put some distance between us and this old place?

"We're not leaving yet," he said, answering my silent question and extinguishing my flicker of hope. "I'm with you on the coffin. But I have to know what, or who, is in there." He turned toward the lit room. My wary eyes followed his gaze, not believing what he was saying.

"Are you f-ing kidding me?" I gasped. Garrett's sense of adventure was getting the best of him, and I was getting nervous about his qualifications as our unspoken leader. Nothing about this place—the fresh graves, the black-covered windows, the freshly dug up coffin sitting on an abandoned church's pulpit—was telling a story that I wanted to hear, much less be a part of.

"What?" he asked, meeting my bewildered stare with a serious one of his own. "Could be a runaway for all we know. Or runaways."

The moment he made the word "runaway" plural, I understood. Didn't agree with him, but I understood. Garrett had the missing girls on his mind. He was thinking about *them*, not us, and thinking they might be hiding out in this church. Hoping so, most likely. Who wouldn't want to be the one to solve the mystery and actually find the girls? I understood completely.

But I didn't buy the idea that it was them. There were too many screwed up aspects of this no-longer vacant church to be a simple hideout for a group of teenage runaways. The coffin changed things. It was obvious to me that something bad was taking place here, and I couldn't believe he wasn't seeing it.

"Garrett," I whispered, trying to keep my voice down, but using his name for emphasis, "you can't be serious. Megan, Hannah and Becca, they're not here. I don't know where they are, but they sure as hell aren't hiding out in this deserted church, digging up graves from the cemetery and bringing the coffins inside. Are you kidding me?"

"I know, I know," he said, talking to me, but keeping his eyes on the room with the light. The way the room's doorway was positioned, not much was visible from our vantage point. There was a section of dingy white wall, but beyond that, anything could have been in there.

Or anyone.

"But, there still might be a connection," he continued. "Wouldn't you like to find out if they're here? This could be the break the police need."

"But, we're twenty miles from New Paris," I pointed out. "There are a hundred places between here and there they could hide out in."

"If that's what they're doing, which I doubt," I argued back, feeling more certain on this point than on anything I'd said in my life. "And what are the odds that we stumbled upon the very place so far from home that —"

"Okay!" Garrett interrupted, his voice threatening to hit a dangerous level. "But, someone's here. Or has been here. And it's a hell of a coincidence when you think about it."

I stood in the near darkness and found myself shaking my head and feeling like I'd been here before. The conversation was much the same as the one we'd had on the driveway after finding the freshly dug graves. And like that conversation, Garrett had piqued my interest despite the voice inside me yelling "no" like I was about to jump off a ledge. The idea of finding the answer to the missing girls, or the girls themselves, was definitely appealing. We'd be heroes. Heck, the town would probably hold a parade in our honor. Not only did I think he was barking up the wrong tree, but also, we weren't equipped with the tools to handle what we might find if we investigated further. I had a downright bad feeling about doing anything in this place beyond running out of it. But Garrett stood, waiting for me to answer.

"Alright," I sighed. "We peek inside the room, then we get the hell out of here. No matter what is or isn't in there. If it's nothing, we leave just the same as if there is something. No more private investigator bullshit. We get the hell out of here, tell the cops about this place, and let them decide whether or not what's going on here is as fucked up as it looks. Deal?"

"Deal," Garrett said with a single nod. There was no smile on his face this time. No swagger. The cockiness was gone, leaving only commitment. It wasn't about an adventure anymore, and I should have recognized that earlier. He was just as scared as I was. I could see it in his alert eyes, open slightly wider than normal. This was just Garrett wanting to do whatever he could to help. Basically, Garrett being Garrett.

And truthfully, that was one of the main reasons I called him my best friend.

"Alright, Dickhead," I said, "let's go check it out."

Bone 20 White

She laid on her frameless bed, trying to soothe the dull pain growing behind her right eye. It was the same pain, in the same place, about once a week or so. It was enough to make her eye water. The pain. Sometimes she could get it to go away if she tried hard enough. If she relaxed and hummed her song. Not just any song, but her favorite. It always soothed her pain and calmed her when she was feeling nervous. Just like her mother used to do.

Softly, and with eyes closed, she started to hum the tune. It was the same melody her mother had often sung to her as she tucked the blanket underneath her chin and planted downy kisses on her forehead when she was little. She could still recall her mother's gentle voice, like an angel's, drifting over her like the golden slumbers of which she sang. Lulling her toward the land of dreams. Until the last thing she would remember before drifting off was her mother's voice floating toward her from her bedroom doorway. Just before her mother clicked off the light, just before she –

Her eyes flew open like she'd been poked with a stick. Her muscles tensed as she realized her mistake. Her stupid, stupid mistake. She had forgotten to put out the candles in the classroom. Her father had warned her about that before. About leaving candles burning. Warned her and followed through on his threats more than once.

Rolling off the mattress, her feet hit the floor running. She ducked underneath the curtain and scaled her father's mattress, scooting her bottom across it in one long slide, until she was on her feet again approaching the doorway. She had to get to the classroom before her father. Her hand went to her right eye, remembering. She just had to.

Bone 21 White

We crept between the ragged and tortured pews, slowly slinking past the long shadows toward the room with the light. The possibilities of what we might find in there ran through my mind on a loop. The missing girls. A homeless vagrant. Remnants of a Satanic ritual. As we crossed over the center aisle that divided the sanctuary lengthwise in half, I tried to focus on my favorite possibility: the missing girls. A harmless homeless guy just looking to stay dry and remain undisturbed ran a close second. As we made our way closer to the doorway, I crossed my proverbial fingers for the best, but braced myself for the worst.

We were only a few steps from the room when another sound came from above. Halting our forward motion, we were forced flat against the wall. On our way across the large room, Garrett had pointed out the stairway that led up to a second story. My eyes went right to it then. Maybe it was a wild animal—squirrel, raccoon, bird—but there was definitely *something* making the sounds. Something more than just the wind.

The shuffling continued, sounding even more like an animal scurrying across the floor than before. Nothing more than that, I told myself and exhaled the air I'd been holding when the shuffling stopped. While I rested my back against the wall on one side of the doorway, Garrett took up position on the other. We looked more like a couple of S.W.A.T. officers about to raid a crack house than two half-frightened teenagers about to investigate a room simply because a light was on. I looked at Garrett, and in true cop show fashion, he looked back at me and nodded.

The room was empty except for six miniature chairs placed side by side in the middle with one larger, adult-sized chair facing them. On each of the tiny chairs was a tattered doll, positioned to face the large chair and the chalkboard hanging crookedly on the wall behind it. The whole room wasn't much more than a coat closet. For all I knew, it could have been one in a previous life.

After another look at Garrett to make sure I wasn't going in alone, we stepped farther into the room and were fully embraced by the light. The room was warm, whether it was heat from the three nearly consumed candles glowing on a narrow stand in the corner or the presence of recent body heat. Either way, it felt good on my damp face. I was chilled to the bone and this was the first heat I'd been exposed to since stepping out of the cab of Garrett's truck, not to mention the first real light since the sun had been swallowed up by storm clouds.

With thoughts of warming my frigid hands on their enticing flames, I made a beeline for the candles, but the notion escaped me before I'd made it even halfway across the room. The gears of my brain ground against each other at what I saw to my right. I took a couple of steps closer.

Random paper drawings of houses, stick figure families, cats, dogs and turtles clung to the chipped and cracked plaster wall with thin strips of clear tape. Drawn using all the colors from a Crayola 64 box, the drawings themselves were simple and caused little reason for concern. Where the concern came into play, however, was with the names that were scrawled on the papers in what appeared to be a child's hand. Each drawing was signed with a name, and each name was the same as one of the missing girls from New Paris.

Megan.

Hannah.

Becca.

My heart trilled for a moment at the thought of having found them, but as I looked closer at the drawings, my delight descended into uneasiness. Four drawings each were attributed to Megan and Hannah, while only two bore Becca's name. But judging by the skill level displayed in the drawings, they weren't drawn by seniors in high school. They weren't terrible, but the attention to detail wasn't there. Hannah Rogers was a very gifted artist whose paintings and drawings had always won awards at the local art shows. Despite her name being on them, I knew that Hannah couldn't have drawn these clumsy crayon pictures. Still, the fact that I found their names on something in this place set off every alarm in my mind.

I turned to Garrett hoping he could offer a plausible explanation, although I couldn't imagine what that might be. But Garrett stood in the middle of the room, jaw hung slightly open, staring at the chalk board on the wall. By the look on his face, he'd also seen something that wasn't quite right, and depending on what it was, I had a feeling I might regret having seen the drawings. Basically, I had limitations. I could only handle so much and was already approaching that line.

I forced my eyes to follow his, and for the first time since entering the room, really took notice of the chalkboard. Or, more specifically, what was written on it in pink chalk. From top to bottom and side to side, like a schoolboy's punishment, was one sentence written over and over:

For the hour to reap has come, for the harvest of the earth is fully ripe.

"What the...?" was all I could get out as I stood there mesmerized by the words. They had little meaning for me, but dread poured into every inch of my body. *Reap. Harvest.* The words kept jumping out at me, drawing my eyes back to them every time I tried to look away. I was at a loss. I felt like a stoner standing in the potato chip aisle, unable to decide which variety would best satisfy the munchies.

"Creepy shit," Garrett said. His head was slowly nodding up and down, and I wasn't even sure he was aware of it.

"That ain't all," I said as the rhythmic pounding of my heart sounded in my ears. "I'd tell you what I saw on the wall over there, but after seeing this, I don't want to take the time. I just wanna get the hell outta here. I'm officially done with this place." I patted Garrett on the back as I started to walk past him, and was admittedly thankful when he turned to fall in beside me. No more arguments. No more persuasion. Garrett was just as freaked as I was. Once we got back to town, we'd tell the police about this place. It'd be their problem then and maybe it would still lead to wherever the girls were. In any case, we'd never have to see this creepy church again.

As soon as we stepped into the openness of the sanctuary we were greeted with an audible gasp, the sound of someone's breath catching in surprise. I stopped in mid-stride and looked back at Garrett. His eyes were equally wide, probing mine. It took only a second for us to realize that neither of us has made the alerted sound, and the hairs on the back of my neck prickled.

We scanned the sanctuary from where we'd frozen and saw nothing. Maybe we had imagined the sound. A sigh of relief was escaping my lips when a soft whimper spun us in the direction of the stairway. A teenage girl stood barefoot in the middle of the stairs like she was just on her way down. She wore grey sweat pants rolled up over her calves and a maroon NPHS cheerleading t-shirt, both of which looked like they hadn't been washed in weeks. She was dressed the way the New Paris cheerleaders dressed when they weren't in uniform, but this girl was far from a New Paris cheerleader. Stringy yellow hair, dull and thin, hung from her desolate scalp. Her gaunt face, filthy and pockmarked from acne run amuck, offered not even a hint of beauty. One eye looked normal, but the other was only slightly open as she looked down in shock at the two of us.

"No!" she screamed, as if we had brought her worst nightmare to life. "You're not supposed to be here! You're not!"

Garrett and I exchanged the same glance. *What the hell?*

As always, Garrett took the lead by putting his hands out in a calming fashion.

"Are you okay?" he asked the girl, taking a single step in her direction. Her face tightened further. She looked at us in horror as she took a step back, rising up onto the step behind her.

"Who are you?" I asked, not knowing what else to do. The back part of my brain was telling me what we should do, screaming it, actually. It was demanding we do what we should have been doing all along. Unfortunately, my feet wouldn't comply.

Garrett raised his hand higher in an attempt to assure the girl we wouldn't harm her. As he did, the rigid fear seemed to drain from the girl's body like air escaping a punctured lung. As the muscles in her taut face relaxed, a quiet resolve seemed to come over her features as quickly as they'd appeared. Now she stood defiant, looking at us like we hadn't really scared her at all, like our encounter was all part of some grand plan. The transformation was as strange as just about anything else I'd seen since stepping foot in the church.

"Who are you?" Garrett asked, restating my question.

"His daughter," she said matter-of-factly. Too much so for my taste. Like we were supposed to know who the hell she was referring to.

"His daughter?" Garrett repeated. He shot me a look of uncertainty. Then, when all I could do was shrug my shoulders, he turned back to the girl. "Whose daughter?"

It was as if she were already growing tired of dealing with the two of us. Her gaze shifted from us to something farther back in the church. A faint smile pulled at her lips, and her arm came up stiffly at the shoulder. With a subtle twitch of her wrist and a full-on smirk, she pointed.

"His."

I didn't have time to turn around. I didn't have time to see what or who she was pointing at. In fact, I'd barely heard the whooshing sound of something flying through the air before the sudden thump at the base of my skull caused everything to go black.

Bone **22** White

Her heart was beating so fast, she thought she would pass out. Her face was flushed and she felt like she needed to sit down. She dropped onto the edge of her mattress, sat with her legs stretched out on the floor and tried to breathe. Lips quivering, she hummed her song. Hummed and hummed, bouncing her leg so fast, it threatened to throw off the tempo of her tune.

Neither the humming nor the bouncing helped. She laid back, arms at her sides, and stared at the intricate spider webs flanking the corners of the ceiling. Inky shadows played across the walls, created by the pale 40-watt bulb of the small lamp on the dresser she shared with her father. It wasn't really a dresser at all, but an old lectern podium that was hollow in the middle. Her father had built shelves into the center of it, calling it a dresser, which worked just fine since the bedroom wasn't really a bedroom.

She closed her eyes, blocking out the only light Father allowed with any regularity, and tried to concentrate on the tapping of the rain against the lone window of the loft. She was rarely allowed to leave the premises, and her imagination was well-honed from spending so much time alone. Using her creative skills now, she could almost decipher a calming melody inside all the tapping. If she listened closely. Could just make it out. She concentrated on the music of the rain, added it to the humming of her song and breathed. And after a couple of minutes, she finally felt herself start to relax.

She did not scare easily. Not anymore. She was only frightened now because her father had looked scared. And he didn't scare easily, either. In fact, this was probably the first time she had ever seen him that way. In her life. Not even that morning when her mommy had given him a ride. Taken him to the place with the barbed wire. *Prison.* She hated that word. Didn't like saying it. All the kids at school told her it meant bad things and was for bad people. She was very young at the time, but she remembered it. Remembered the day. The day another daddy went away.

Thankfully he had come back for her. Wanted to be together. She hoped it was forever this time, but now she was worried.

"I'm not going back," he'd spat before ordering her up to her room. "Ain't never going back."

And the look in his eyes. She'd seen it. Something that she had seen in eyes before, just not in her father's. It was the look in her mother's eyes when her father had returned from that word she didn't like to say. Fear and dread. Almost like the eyes could see the future and knew something was coming.

Something bad.

Bone 23 White

The back of my head throbbed. That's what I noticed first and foremost as I came out of the fog. It literally felt like I'd been hit with a shovel. Maybe I had. The second thing I noticed was the pressure under my arms. And a sense of movement. I was gliding across a hardwood floor, albeit not willingly. I was being dragged. The heels of my tennis shoes would bounce when they encountered a loose board or the edge of a hymnal wedged against a pew. I blinked a couple times and shook my aching head until my senses started to clear.

"Dude," I said, wincing when the back of my ankles cracked against something hard. A step maybe, but my head was spinning too much for me to make much sense of my surroundings in the dark. "What happened?"

When Garrett didn't answer, I looked down at the fingertips sticking out from underneath my armpits. The nails were black with dirt, grime and who knew what else. Cracked and raw knuckles swelled like knots at the bone joints. They were the rough and calloused hands of someone who used them to earn a living. Beyond that, they were the largest, ugliest fingers I'd ever seen.

They weren't Garrett's hands.

When I struggled against their grip, the pressure only tightened. Before I could do much in the way of struggling free, I felt myself being hoisted into the air. Looking down, my already dire circumstances worsened. The black hole of the coffin, its lid now propped open, waited to swallow me up. A candle had been placed at the head of the coffin, and in its murky light I could see clothes, drab and threadbare, mounded in piles along the edges of the wooden box's interior.

Without even a grunt, the large hands twisted me in the air and threw me in the coffin like a bag of laundry. I landed face down, my chest absorbing most of the energy. Before I could turn myself over, the lid slammed shut, almost crushing my leg. And for the second time in only a few minutes, my world went dark.

Bone 24 White

Her heartbeats had finally slowed by the time she rose to pace the floor. The wooden floorboards between the mattresses were loose and felt rough on her bare feet. *What had just happened? Who were the two boys? What were they doing here?* No one had entered the church in months. Not since she'd been here. Not voluntarily, at least.

Father always warned her about strangers, and what might happen if someone were to ever come snooping around their new home. They'd take him away from her, he'd said. Again. She looked over at the dark green canvas bag, packed and sitting beside the dresser. Just in case. Father always said they had to be ready, just in case. An uneasy shudder ran through her and she tried to shake the thought from her mind. She liked it here. It had taken some time, but she had gotten used to the isolation of the church in the woods. Liked it, even. It finally felt like home. She did not want to leave.

A sharp sound came from outside, different from the droning clamor of the storm. It wasn't a loose shingle flapping in the wind this time. It wasn't a limb from the big, ugly tree out back slapping against the side of the building. This was a loud bang. Loud enough to be heard clearly through the wind and rain.

She tried to resist but within a couple of seconds, her curiosity had already gotten the better of her, and she switched off the lamp. On her hands and knees, she crawled over to the only window in the loft and pulled the black curtain to the side, but, only a couple inches. Just enough. It was all she dared. The window had been given a thick coat of black paint, but she'd managed to scrape a small hole with her fingernail awhile back. She didn't like going against Father's rules. She knew she'd be punished if he found out, but just this one thing. Just a small hole. The size of a penny. On her knees, she put her eye to the opening and looked out at the dark world.

The light mounted on the shed spotlighted her father in the weak pool of light. He was dragging something, and it didn't take long for her to recognize one of the boys as the something he was dragging. It was the one in the red jacket and the sound had been the shed door slamming open. Her father walked backward into the outbuilding, pulling him inside until the red jacket disappeared. The boy's legs laid in the mud for a moment, long enough for her to begin wondering what sorts of things awaited the boy in the shed. She slid her tongue across her rough bottom lip as she thought. Surely her father planned to harvest him, but which tools would he use? She had her favorites. After a moment, the boy's legs were swallowed up by the shed's mouth, followed by his feet until ultimately, he was gone from the night altogether. With a shrug, she allowed the black curtain to drop back into place.

Whether it was the constant pitter-patter of the rain, or the fact that all she'd put in her stomach that day was a bowl of chicken broth and several glasses of water, the insistence of a full bladder made itself known. Urgently. As if she'd been holding it for days. She *needed* to use the bathroom, but doubt clouded her mind. Father had sent her upstairs with strict orders to shut the door and stay put. She didn't know if she was allowed. Disobeying her father led to punishment, and she remembered each of the times he'd had to punish her. Remembered them well. Her eye, she was sure, would never be the same. But surely he didn't mean that she couldn't use the bathroom. Surely that was allowed.

Quietly, she slipped over to the door and placed her ear against the cool wood. No sounds were coming from the other side. Other than the effects of wind and rain on its outside, the inside of the church was still. Making as little noise as possible, she twisted the tarnished brass knob to the left until she heard a clicking sound, then pulled open the door ever so slightly.

As she peered down the darkened stairway, she scolded herself for going so slowly. She knew she didn't have much time. Her father could be returning very soon, so she had to hurry. She had to pee so badly. And even as the question entered her mind, she assured herself that her eagerness had nothing to do with her curiosity about what had happened to the other boy. About what Father had done with him. Nope. Nothing at all.

Bone 25 White

Cat urine. The overwhelming stench of it permeated my consciousness, and I was suddenly alert – to the stench, to where I was, to the circumstances I'd so abruptly found myself in. I'd seen stories on the news of people in harrowing situations. Stories where people would say, "I thought I was gonna die." I'd never understood the concept: to think you were going to die. Yet, here I was, trapped in a coffin thinking I was going to die. It was a strange sensation. Not at all what I imagined it would feel like. But, now I understood what the people on the news understood. I was calm, not anxious. Thoughtful, not frantic. Hell, for all I knew I was still suffering from the groggy aftereffects of being knocked over the head. My knowledge of coffins was limited, but what I knew for sure was that I wasn't in a hurry to be in one. Yet here I was.

I struggled to maneuver myself inside the oversized litter box. I was sharing the coffin with numerous piles of old clothing. At least, I assumed they were old. The mustiness was the one smell I could detect over the cat piss. Though the tight space made it difficult, I inched my body around until I was lying flat on my back.

In the absolute darkness, my thoughts jettisoned back to the empty grave we'd seen in the old cemetery beside the driveway. The image of the open grave loomed before my eyes, so real I could touch it … or fall into it. That image, along with the knowledge of where I was lying, sent shivers through me and brought bile up the back of my throat. This coffin had recently been buried underground with a dead body in it. For nearly a hundred years, it had been buried and all that remained now were the clothes. What happened to the body? *The remains.* Why would anyone want it? And why the hell was the once buried coffin sitting in a church?

As each question entered my mind, my heart rate escalated. My skin prickled like millions of phantom spiders were crawling all over my body. The growing fear drew tears to the corners of my eyes. I fought to stave them off as I lay there on my back, ironically in the same position as the corpse that had occupied the coffin before me. But, what I couldn't fight off was the next thought that entered my head. *Was this my coffin now?*

The calm I'd felt earlier had officially been shot to hell. Still, with my eyes squeezed shut, I tried to compose myself. I willed my breaths to come slower. My heart rate to decelerate. It took a few minutes, but eventually, I was cool-headed again and could think.

The first clear thought was that I needed a plan. One thing that I'd learned from years of both successful and not so successful fishing was that all my success came when I had a good plan. And each step of the plan was as important as the others. The first step in catching a fish was to determine what kind of fish you wanted to catch. Once that was decided, you had to figure out where the best place to catch that fish would be, and focus on it. What time of day, what type of weather would lend itself to greater success? Once all of that was figured out, it generally came down to gear. What tackle or bait would attract the elusive fish? What would it be in the mood for? And at the end of the day, if you executed each step successfully, there was a good chance you'd be having fish for dinner that night. You might even have enough to invite a few friends over. The plan was everything.

I needed a plan.

The first strategic step in my new plan was to open my eyes. It was dark. I couldn't see anything. But after a moment, my eyes adjusted, and inside the blackness, the thinnest sliver of light slid between the lid and the bottom of the coffin. The wood must have warped in the decades it spent underground, because these things were usually sealed up pretty tight. The crack in the wood wasn't large enough to shed any real light. It was just enough to notice.

The next step that came to mind wasn't exactly ingenious, but it was the most natural move for someone in my situation to make. I pressed my hands firmly against the lid and pushed with everything I had. Under the strain, my arms – hell, my entire body quivered, violent and painful tremors wracked my head. The large tendon in my wrist pulsated and threatened to snap, but the lid didn't open. It didn't even budge. I slammed an elbow against the lid in frustration. I hadn't expected it to do the trick either, and I wasn't proven wrong. The only thing I got for my efforts was a resounding thud that echoed inside the hollow confines. No doubt the lid was locked or secured somehow.

I considered checking my cell phone for service, but waved it off as soon as the thought entered my mind. I'd used the phone in the mudroom and there was no signal then. There wasn't any reason to believe that I'd have one inside this wooden box. If anything, there was less of a chance now.

I exhaled firmly and willed myself to think. I wasn't sure how long I'd been in the coffin. I wasn't sure if I'd blacked out. The shot I'd taken to the back of my head hurt pretty bad. I'd probably been struck hard enough to black out, but not hard enough to cause any memory loss, or forget where I was. I knew exactly where I was: in a hellish, stinking coffin cloaked in a nightmare. What I didn't know were why I was here, who had done it and what the hell had happened to Garrett.

Bone 26 White

Tap.

The knock against the coffin's lid was faint, yet resounded enough to jolt me nearly upright. My head banged on the coffin lid, sending me back into the moldy, dank cushion of the old clothes. I laid there, motionless. Except for the rising and falling of my chest, everything in my world was still.

"Who's there?" I asked the silence, but no answer followed. My mind raced through the possibilities, Garrett being the obvious one or at least the one I most hoped for. Could it be one of the missing girls? Doubtful. Other than their names on the drawings, there was no evidence that the missing girls had ever been here. The young woman from the stairway had probably drawn them, and could have very well heard their names from the news. So what the hell was she doing here? And who else was in the church with her? The questions tumbled through my head until the tapping came again. This time twice.

"Garrett?" I asked, fingers crossed. But like the first time, I got no response. The silence made me restless, adding even more uncertainty to an already strange situation, and that didn't sit well with me. They had to hear. Someone was toying with me, and once again, my heart rate started to increase. Any early hope that it was Garrett tapping on the lid had faded. He would have responded after realizing it was me inside the coffin, and I'd be well on my way to getting out by now. At the very least, he would have answered.

"Who are you?" I shouted, making absolutely sure I was heard, not that I doubted that I was earlier. "Why are you doing this?" As the echo of my words faded within the casket, the silence outside it grew. It was in that quiet that my fear started to change. Fear wasn't doing me any good. Fear hadn't changed anything. Anger was rising inside me now, fighting back the tears and threatening to take over. Anger might not get me anywhere, either, but it felt a whole hell of a lot better. Liberating. The transformation surprised me, but pleasantly so. In fact, I was about to shout again, rage against whoever was out there, when a faint and muffled voice entered through the crack in the wood.

"It's me. His daughter," the voice said softly.

Again with the "his daughter" bullshit, like I was supposed to know who *he* was. Captive or not, I was in no mood for guessing games. What was happening to me was no game by any stretch.

"What's your name?" I asked, working to keep the edge from creeping into my voice. I remembered how frightened she'd been of us and didn't want to scare her away. That strange girl was my only connection to the outside world.

My question remained unanswered so I gave it another try. This time being as clear as I possibly could.

"What…is…your…name?"

"I'm his daughter."

His daughter.

That was it. I couldn't control the outburst that followed. I slammed my fists into the coffin lid, ignoring the pain ripping through my white knuckles. The heels of my tennis shoes pounded the wood beneath me as I kicked it in frustration. A full on tantrum. And just like a child, I even screamed with all I had, the bulging veins in my neck be damned.

"What is your fucking name?"

I continued thrashing around, wasting a lot of energy. I couldn't help myself. Fear and rage had become one animal, replacing common sense and rationality. Violent energy bubbled up inside me, demanding to be released.

I kept going for a good ten or fifteen seconds. When that energy was finally spent, my aching hands fell to my sides. My tight shoulders sagged and my entire body went limp from exertion. Sweat mixed with tears and ran down my cheeks, into my hair. Despite how good it felt to get it out, none of this was doing me any good. I needed to maintain control and think. I tried to relax, slow my heart rate and just listen. Eyes closed, I breathed deeply through my nose until I felt the tightness in my temples start to loosen. I noticed that all was quiet outside the coffin once again. *Damn it!* I'd scared the girl off.

The silence settled around me like fallen leaves until finally, I heard a whisper. "I'm not sure."

The words came so softly, so hushed I wasn't sure I'd even heard them. It could have been my mind playing tricks on me, for all I knew. Hearing what I wanted to hear. "Not sure of what?" I asked loudly in case it had been real.

"I'm not sure what my name is," the girl answered. She was real, but her statement threw me, and I didn't know how to respond. I took a moment to try and understand, but I just didn't. Was it even possible? Could someone her age, a teenager, *not* know their own name? But, the more I thought about it, the more the reality of the situation told me it was possible. In fact, these circumstances were just screwed up enough for anything to be possible.

"Can you let me out?" I asked. I was sure I knew the answer, but much like giving the lid a shove earlier, it didn't hurt to try. The silence from my new friend gave me a spark of hope. She was considering it.

"No." The flat tone stamped the spark cold.

"Please," I pleaded, elbowing away a wad of filthy clothing that I had just noticed was touching my arm. "Please let me out."

"I can't. He would be so angry."

Even in the darkness, my eyes still shut down. My chin trembled. I was getting nowhere. The anger inside me was receding and fear was settling back into the void left behind. The girl was not going to let me out of the coffin. But I couldn't give up. Maybe, just maybe, she could help in another way. I needed some answers, at least, some reasoning behind it all. With understanding comes possibilities. And I needed some possibilities.

Most of all, I needed a reason to hope.

"Why is he doing this?" But, as soon as the question passed my lips, I realized something. The "why" didn't even matter. The "why" was pointless. The fact was it was happening regardless of why. The real question was how was I going to get out of it.

Patience. With understanding comes possibilities.

"It's his work," the girl answered after a moment.

"What is?" I asked. She was talking so low now. Barely above a whisper. I was having trouble hearing her hushed voice through the dense wood. "What is his work?"

"The harvest."

My stomach knotted, remembering the words repeated across the chalkboard. *For the hour to reap has come, for the harvest of the earth is fully ripe.* Every muscle in my body tensed again. Had I heard her correctly?

"Harvest what?" I asked, but she didn't answer. Seconds ticked by like hours, marked only by the beating of my heart and the humid breath from my lungs.

"Bones," came her whisper.

Bones?

"What about bones?" I questioned.

"The harvest," she said again. "He harvests bones."

"But what does he need with bones?" I squeaked out as the all too familiar fear raised my voice an octave higher.

No answer. I waited, being as patient as anyone could in my situation. The last thing I could afford was to scare her off. Given this new information, I needed this lifeline now more than ever.

"Does he want my bones?" I asked. The question came out very calmly, perhaps because I couldn't get my head around it. Why would anyone harvest bones? This was either some sick joke ... or just sick.

"I don't know," came the soft voice.

A shuffling sound came from beside the coffin, quickening my pulse. Had she left me? I held my breath and listened until I heard a quiet cough. I imagined she had just sat down on the floor beside the coffin. At least I hoped so. It would be a good sign if I were right. It meant I had her attention, and that was something. An opportunity to build hope.

I raised my head slightly and strained to see something, anything through the slit where the light was filtering in. But, it was still no use.

"You're a boy," she said. "He always uses girls."

Girls.

I'd been so wrapped up in what was happening to me, that I had completely forgotten about the girls and the drawings I'd seen. Despite my own dire situation, I allowed myself a bit of optimism that maybe I had found them. That maybe they were still alive, being held captive somewhere in this church, just like me.

"Uses them for what?" I asked. I wasn't sure I wanted to know, but she'd changed topics and I needed to keep up.

"For the harvest," she said, her voice taking on a sing-song quality.

The harvest. Harvesting bones.

As quickly as it had come, the optimism disappeared, only to be replaced by crushing despair. The girls were dead. Killed for their bones by some sick bastard and his defective daughter.

No. I didn't know that for certain. I needed to hold onto to at least some degree of hope.

"The girls," I started, refusing to give up. "Do you know where they are? Megan, Hannah and Becca? I saw their names in that room. Was that you?"

The echo of my words faded without an answer, only a soft humming sound remained. A few bars in, I recognized the tune, and that's when my hands balled into fists, the muscles in my jaw set, and the anger returned stronger than before. The girl was humming a lullaby. I couldn't believe it! I was locked inside this fucking coffin, with her telling me about her deranged father's bone collection like it was a common hobby everyone indulged in, and this demented girl was humming a fucking lullaby? The insanity of it shifted something in my brain and I wanted to wrap my hands around "his daughter's" throat. At that moment, I wanted nothing more than to silence her stupid humming.

The thought chilled me. Could I actually do it? Could I wrap my hands around her throat and squeeze until she was silenced? Yes, I could. All doubt disappeared, and the clarity of that truth shined bright. If I ever got the chance, I could kill this girl. I actually wanted to, in fact. I'd do it because of what was being done to me. What was undoubtedly being done to Garrett and may have already been done to the girls. The realization of my capabilities both empowered *and* scared me.

"What did he do with the girls?" I asked, this time failing to keep the anger out of my voice. There simply was no hiding it now. But, the humming continued, and I still wasn't given an answer to my question, which only pissed me off more. What the hell was she doing? Playing with me? Trying to torment me? Or was she really just so screwed up that she didn't even realize how very wrong all of this was? As much as I tried to give her the benefit of the doubt, I found that very hard to believe.

"Where is he?" I asked, the fury in my voice surprising even me. "I want to talk to him!"

Finally, the childlike humming stopped. Just like that, the agitation I felt softened just slightly, and for a second, I was afraid I was going to get my wish. I didn't know if that would be a good thing or not. Then, that familiar voice returned. That voice with a little too much matter-of-factness in it.

"He went out to the shed. To get some tools."

And for the first time since the conversation started, I regretted getting an answer. *Get some tools?* The images of red hot tongs and rusty saws racing through my head were cut off quickly by another voice, *his* voice.

"You better not be in there, girl," he growled from somewhere in the distance. "Better not be meddling in my work." The booming voice seemed to be coming closer. It carried more menace than any I'd ever heard. "You know what happens when you disobey me!"

I heard the girl scramble to her feet. And just as quickly, my anger faded. I wanted to shout out to her, plead with her not to go, but the threatening tone of the man's voice stopped me.

Moments later, the lonely sound of her feet padding away was accompanied by the nerve-rattling cadence of a hammer striking a nail.

Bone 27 White

She leaned her back against the door and tried to catch her breath for the second time in an hour. She'd been so wrapped up in talking to the boy in the coffin that she hadn't even heard Father come back inside. He would have been so mad if he'd caught her. The very thought of his punishments made her wince. She wasn't even supposed to be downstairs, much less talking to that boy. But he hadn't seen her. Only suspected.

That boy. It was his fault. The first boy she'd talked to since she'd stopped going to school. Easily over a year now. Maybe two. She wished she'd been able to talk to him longer. Find out more about him. Ask him his name. Not that it mattered. It was better not knowing. That's what Father told her. Names only complicated things, made things harder.

Still.

It was true, what she told the boy. She hadn't lied. She really didn't know her name anymore. She knew what her name used to be. Everyone use to call her "Belinda." Her grandfather had called her that before he died, her mother before she went away. The teachers at the school where she used to go. All called her by that name. Belinda. But, for a while now, Father had been calling her "Rosemarie." Her mother's name. For a couple of months now, ever since she'd gotten her monthly visitor. That's what he occasionally called her when he first started crawling into her bed some nights. Now, he called her Rosemarie all the time. Whispering it in her ear as he cuddled with her, then louder when he was between her legs.

She walked over to their makeshift dresser and let her finger trace the spot in the dust where her mother's picture used to sit. Before Father got rid of it. Around the same time he started lying with her. The frame was still in one of her drawers, though, along with her mother's assortment of makeup and perfumes. She wasn't about to get rid of any of it. Never would. She missed her mother. Wished she would come back. Her mother had just up and disappeared one day. Father had been out of *that place* for only a couple weeks. Personally, she had been happy to have him back. She'd already lost one father. But, her mother had been uneasy with his return. And there were the fights. The oh-so scary fights.

The only good times during those weeks were early in the mornings when Father was still asleep. She would shuffle into the kitchen in her pink princess pajamas and white fuzzy slippers with those raccoon eyes that she hoped to never grow out of. Her mother could usually be found at the table, drinking a cup of coffee and reading one of her dirty books. At least that's what her father called them. *Dirty books.* The ones with the beautiful men and women on the cover. They always looked so in love. She often wondered if her mother had ever felt the way the people on the cover looked. She doubted it. Doubted it very much.

And then one morning, she'd gone into the kitchen, but her mother wasn't there. Her mother wasn't anywhere. That was the same morning Father made her pack. Only what she could carry, he'd said. Then he brought her to the church. Their new home. She had the run of the old church, but he made a big deal about keeping the door to the basement locked. A few days later, the dark curtains appeared over the freshly painted windows. She'd been sad when that happened. When the pretty stained glass disappeared beneath a layer of black. It wasn't until several months later that he started leaving the basement door unlocked. It tempted her, which was probably his plan, but she never bit. Eventually, he took her down with him and showed her what he spent so much time doing.

His work.

She'd been terrified at first. Repulsed. Vomited more than once. But then the lessons began and there was no more time for that foolishness. Now she understood the importance of what Father did. Must do. It was how they survived. A simple hunter providing for his family. For her. Because she was now his only family.

With her fingertip, she drew a heart in the dust on top of the dresser and allowed a grin to pull at her cheeks. Her mother used to draw hearts on things just to let Belinda know she loved her and was thinking about her. The bathroom mirror in red waxy lipstick. The napkins she would pack in her lunch before sending her off to school.

Slowly, the grin faded. Those days were gone. And so was her mother. With the same finger that had just drawn the heart, she drew a large X over it. Then, not wanting her father to see either, she wiped the whole thing clean with the edge of her hand. In its wake, it left a sweeping path of brown wood showing through the layer of grey dust.

She shivered from the isolation of being very much alone, then shook her head. It was a silly thought. She was far from alone. The church was more full now than it had been in years. Definitely more full than it had been since she'd arrived. It housed people again. A congregation even. Besides just her and her father, there was now someone in the shed out back. Someone in that dirty coffin in the big room.

And then there was the basement…

Bone 28 White

The hammering had stopped within the hour, by my best guess, and the church had gone quiet. I'd lain still for a long time, not knowing where the man was, until my thoughts drifted to the missing girls. Were they being held somewhere in this church, too? Had Megan, Hannah or Becca spent time in this very coffin? I shifted my body and something jabbed at my leg. It was only then that I remembered I had a pair of needle nose pliers in the lower pocket of my cargo shorts.

Anytime I went fishing, I carried a pair of needle nose pliers in my pocket, just in case a fish swallowed the hook and I needed to retrieve the barbed piece of metal from its gullet. It was good practice. Most fishermen carried a pair in their tackle box, at least. I, however, carried mine in my pocket, because I seemed to always need them handy. More often than not, actually. If I caught ten fish, eight of them would probably have swallowed the hook. I often wondered if I was doing something wrong, but Garrett didn't do anything different, so I had no way to tell.

I wrestled my hand down into my pocket until I felt the familiar rubber of the orange handles. Once my fingers wrapped around them, I let out the deep breath I'd been holding ever since remembering the pliers. I pulled them out of my pocket and held them in front of my face. I couldn't really make out their profile in the darkness of the coffin, but just holding them was enough to restore some sense of optimism, something that had been significantly fading over the last hour. Lord knows what I was going to do with the pliers. I just knew that having them was certainly better than *not* having them.

Scenarios involving the pointed tool began running through my mind. I imagined myself stabbing the man in the eye with them when he opened the coffin. Ramming them through his hand as he went to grab at me, possibly even pinning his hand to the side of the coffin and giving me a chance to get away. Maybe even drive them into his chest and end this whole ordeal right then and there.

If the circumstances hadn't been so dire, my situation so frightening, I probably would have smiled at my thuggish posturing. I would never be confused with a tough guy. I'd never even been in a fight, but I could feel something changing in me with every passing minute I spent in that coffin. Dark thoughts suddenly seemed normal. Thoughts of violence. It was a realization, really, of what I could and would do, if need be. And those thoughts were birthed by one thing and one thing only.

The will to survive.

After plotting out a few more ghastly scenarios befitting a Tarantino movie, another idea entered my mind that wasn't violent at all, but much more practical, at least in my present circumstances. Maybe I could use the pliers to get myself out of the coffin before the guy even came back. This should have been my first thought but, like a psycho in a hockey mask, murderous thoughts were now coming all too easily to me.

I laid the pliers on my chest and ran my hands along the seam between the wooden coffin and its lid, searching for locks, hinges, anything. Maybe I could use the pliers to unscrew some bolts, or pull some pins. Whatever it was that was holding the lid secure. But, as my fingers explored the ins and outs of the coffin, I didn't find anything like that. Just lengths of brittle silk that had long since lost its luxuriousness. And the occasional splinter.

I tried thinking back to any experiences I'd had with coffins. I'd been to two funerals in my life. One was my grandfather's on my dad's side, and the other was for an old neighbor who used to yell at me for stealing raspberries off of his prized plants. Both funerals had one thing in common, other than the fact I had to borrow ties from my dad that were too long: the lids on the caskets were split across the top. The bottom half remained closed, concealing the legs, while the other half was propped open, revealing the deceased from the waist up. So I changed gears and searched for the seam that divided the lid into two sections.

As my hands searched through the darkness like a blind person reading Braille, the decayed silk ripped free from the lid with the slightest effort, and I had to keep pushing is aside to reach the wood. It made me wonder just how old the coffin really was. But, as much as I felt around the lid above me, I still didn't find a seam. Apparently, the lid on this coffin didn't split.

An ache settled into my shoulders from the cramped quarters. My muscles were so rigid and tight, it felt like boulders were tied to the base of my neck. I started rotating my shoulders as much as I could in the limited space. Over the next couple of minutes, I relieved some of the stiffness, but the soreness stayed behind.

As I carefully stretched, a thought occurred to me. I don't know where the thought came from, but I wondered if, back in the day, grave robbing was really as much of a problem as old horror movies suggested. Because this coffin had "back in the day" written all over it. If it was indeed a problem back then, there had to be some way of securing the top of the coffin to the bottom in order to prevent it from being easily opened again once it was sealed. A locking mechanism of some sort.

As much as I could, I wiggled and scrunched my body against the back of the coffin and tried to look down the length of the slit where the light was coming through. Around the middle of the coffin, I saw it. Or, at least I saw something. I didn't know if it was exactly what I was looking for, but there was a darkened area, the break in the strip of light I was looking for. My heart rate rose and I could feel my blood start to pump faster in anticipation. It's strange how something as little as seeing that dark spot could have such an effect. But, when you're grasping at straws, even the shortest one is a big deal.

Grabbing a piece of silk from above my head, I tore it free and ripped it into a thin, narrow strip. I carefully tried to slide the flimsy cloth into the narrow crack between the coffin and its lid. I quickly found it to be like trying to thread a needle. It took a few moments, but when I finally got it in, I continued to feed the cloth until I figured there were at least a couple of inches hanging outside the coffin. Like a thief using a credit card on a doorjamb, I slid the piece of silk down the length of the coffin toward the dark spot.

Just as I had hoped, the silk caught on the blockage and wouldn't go any farther. My heart was pounding so loud I had to plead with it to be quiet. It was irrational, I know, but my fear that someone might hear it was real. Before getting too excited, I slid the cloth back away from the dark spot and tried again. It caught just as before. After trying a couple of more times just to be sure, my eyes grew damp and a lump of joy formed in my throat. Maybe, just maybe, I was on the upside of this roller coaster ride. But I steeled myself against being overly optimistic. I wasn't free yet. I'd found what was keeping the lid secure, keeping me locked inside the musty and cramped prison, so at the very least, I was headed in the right direction.

I drew the cloth back inside the coffin so it wouldn't draw any unwanted attention if anyone should happen to walk into the room. I hadn't heard any sounds for awhile, but I was sure the girl and her twisted father were somewhere in the church. At any moment, one or the other could come around. What they would be coming for, I tried not to imagine. But, I knew they weren't keeping me locked up for something as innocuous as a tea party.

He harvests their bones.

I ran my hand along the area where the locking mechanism held the lid closed, hoping to find something made of metal, a casing of some kind that I'd missed earlier. But, just as before, all I felt was wood, nothing different.

Just as doubt crept back in, taunting my growing optimism, another idea formed, and I searched around me for the pliers. After extricating them from some stale clothing or twisted silk—I wasn't sure which—I tried to stick the needle noses into the slit itself. I figured if I could wedge them in, maybe I could use them like a pry bar. The bare edge of the point went in, but slipped right back out when I applied any real pressure. The point was just too big to do what I was asking of it. *Damn it!*

I pushed against the wood in frustration, willing it to give way. It didn't, but a slight cracking sound made my eyes widen. Either the wood of the coffin was thinner around the latch, or there was a void. That cracking sound told me that area wasn't solid like the rest of the coffin and that was a very good sign.

With the pliers held against the thinner wood with one hand, I hit the end of the tool as hard as I could with the palm of my other. The tip dug into the wood like a chisel. After a couple of strikes, the hardened steel point found its way deeper into the softer, dry-rotted wood. The wood splintered, making way for steel. On the fourth try, the nose of the pliers hit something hard and a distinct *ping* rang out. It was an unmistakable sound.

Metal striking metal.

I'd found the locking mechanism. Whether it took minutes or hours, I wasn't sure, but I chipped away a hole about the size of a man's wallet from around the metal box in the wall of the coffin. The mechanism jiggled a bit when I pushed on it, but it was still held in place by the lid. There was a pin or something coming from the top, engaging it to the bottom.

I worked the metal box back and forth with my fingertips, loosening it a little more each time. Eventually, the box was loose enough to fit the tip of the pliers behind it. I pried with the aid of more leverage. With a vicious jolt, the metal box jerked away from the wood where it had been embedded for probably a hundred years. It still hung from its engagement in the top, but the mechanism itself was free.

My heart was pounding from my success as much as the exertion, and I struggled to lie still, just to make sure I hadn't been heard. As my tiny world grew silent once again, I feared that everyone in a three county area had heard my pounding, including the menacing occupants of this church. In comparison, the silence here was so dense, so complete. I allowed myself no other movement but to breathe.

Those were the longest moments of my life. Every second my work went undetected, I debated how long to wait. How long was long enough, and how long was too long? I was so close to busting out of jail, I sure as hell didn't want to miss the opportunity. Nor did I want to burst headlong into a psycho and his hammer.

As the stillness remained, I determined enough time had passed. I placed my palms on the top of the coffin and, with my heart in my stomach, gave it a push. The low groan from the old metal hinges was the sweetest sound I'd heard in a long, long time.

Bone 29 White

The sanctuary was awash in shadows that all blended together to form the darkness. The candles in the makeshift classroom had been snuffed out, reducing the visibility inside the sanctuary to an all-time low. I would need to use my cell phone to get around at all, though I worried about how much longer the battery would last. It could be awhile before I got somewhere with service, and I damn sure needed to have enough power to make a call when I did. Still, I needed to make it out of this room before I could even think about making a run for the safety of civilization.

I stuffed a hand in my pocket for the phone, but found what felt like large granules of sand under my fingertips when I pulled it out. What the heck had gotten into my pocket? When I pressed the power button on the side of the phone, the screen came to life and I saw the source of the sand. Turns out, it wasn't sand at all. The screen was crackled, shattered like the veins on a leaf. Lines crisscrossed the glass in all directions, with small pieces of it missing entirely. The screen was beyond repair, and there still was no signal, but at least the phone wasn't a complete loss. It still provided the soft blue light I needed.

Risking everything, I took a deep breath, then cast the tinted light out into the room. As far as I could tell, neither the man nor his daughter were anywhere in the sanctuary. Not knowing where they were was unsettling, but quite frankly, seeing that creepy girl or her father anywhere near me would have been far more unsettling. I had no idea what I would've done. Or what *they* would have done. I didn't care where they were, just as long as they weren't standing between me and the back door. They could be in the classroom drawing more pictures in crayon and singing duets for all I cared. I was getting the hell out.

I took a deep breath, neither relaxed nor frightened, and prepared myself to escape this hell-hole.

I lifted myself up and out of the coffin, setting my feet on a splintered wooden stage. I could tell by scanning my cell around that pathways were worn in the tired varnish from a long-departed minister who paced over the same area for years. The gaps between the floorboards were wide and the entire platform had definitely seen better days.

As I let go of the side of the coffin, my knees buckled, and I grabbed onto it again to steady myself. I must have spent more time in the wooden box than I'd thought. I shook one leg, and then the other, enduring the unpleasant tingle as the circulation returned. Once I thought I could do it without falling, I took the first wobbly steps toward the mudroom.

Where was Garrett?

I tiptoed across the stage, my thoughts turning to my friend. I should have asked the girl about him when I had the chance, but I'd been too busy with my own problems at the time. I would have felt better if he was there with me. He was the go-to guy in difficult situations. Not me. His escape seemed unlikely. Garrett had been standing right beside me when my life took the turn toward Shitville. There was a chance he'd been spared the same fate, but it was a slight one. There was, after all, only one coffin. Maybe he'd made a run for it and escaped this forsaken place. Or even, it he'd been captured too, there was a chance that Garrett had broken out of his prison before I did. He could very well be on his way to get help.

Before that spark of hope could become a flame, the doubting Thomas in me pointed out just how remote this location was. We had walked for what seemed like miles without coming across a house, car or anything else that might be of assistance. And unless the wind had changed directions one hundred and eighty degrees, blowing toward the docks instead of away from them, he wasn't getting that broken down boat back to the launch ramp anytime soon. So at the very least, even if he did get away, I was looking at some serious wait time before any help would arrive. That thought shot what little hope I had remaining all to hell.

The most likely scenario was that Garrett hadn't gotten away, which would mean he was still somewhere in the church. That presented me with my own twisted version of "Would You Rather?" Run for my life and save my own ass, which was my first instinct, or stick around and try to find my best friend?

As I passed through the doorway and down the two steps into the mudroom, I found the decision had already been made for me. The hammering I'd heard earlier was explained as well. Six thick planks of mismatched wood stretched across the doorframe like bandages on an ugly wound, blocking any route of escape through the door we'd entered through.

Still, I grabbed ahold of one of the planks and pulled. It didn't give at all, just as I expected. Holding up my cell to look closer, I counted at least six large nails in each end of the planks, holding them securely in place. My scrawny arms didn't have the strength to get these boards to budge. I considered finding something strong enough to pry on them until they buckled, splintered apart or stripped out the nails. But, with six boards to get through, that would make way too much noise not to bring someone running. I'd be lucky if I got through the second one before I had company. This was a dead end. We may have come into the church that way, but it sure as hell didn't look like we'd be getting out the same way.

And if things weren't bad enough, my cell phone started blowing up.

Bone 30 White

My heart rate shot through the roof as I fumbled for the button to silence my screaming ringtone. My hands trembled so badly, I nearly dropped the phone. Twice. I had to tuck it in my armpit to muffle the tinny, whizzing sound of fishing line flying out of a reel. It reverberated through the mudroom, as I cowered down beside the grimy washer.

I flipped the cell phone open just as it stopped ringing. What I saw on the screen came as no surprise, but that didn't make it hurt any less.

Missed call: Mom.

Sonofabitch! She'd probably started to worry when I hadn't made my requisite phone call and decided to call me instead. And with that thought rattling around my head, my heart broke. For me. For her. For the fights we'd been having. Because for the first time in weeks, I actually wanted to talk to her. I mean, *really* wanted to talk to her.

I hid beside the filthy appliances, feeling sorry for myself and once again waiting to find out if anyone else in the church had heard anything. The seconds ticked by slowly, but my heart rate didn't match their pace. The urge to call my mother back gripped me, and I decided the risk would be worth it as long as I was able to let her know where I was. She would be on the phone with the cops seconds later, and they would be on their way.

Except I didn't know where I was.

The abandoned road that led us to the church's driveway was probably one of a hundred in the area. I could describe the church itself and offer up the name, but I wasn't sure how long it had been abandoned. Maybe it would ring a bell with someone who knew the area. Maybe that could be enough.

But it wasn't meant to be. Just as I raised the phone to make the call, the meter changed. The signal was gone. I hit the call back button anyway, but the phone did nothing in response. The tiny white X just sat there on the black screen where the bars had been moments before. The phone was mocking me, telling me to try again later. I could almost hear it snickering. The frustration nearly triggered a re-enactment of the tantrum I'd thrown in the coffin. But I refrained. I'd already dodged a bullet with no one hearing the phone go off. I didn't want to tempt fate again. But my self-control didn't make me feel any better.

I got to my feet and climbed back up the steps into the main room, shaking my head at how close I'd come to outside contact, and cursing myself for letting it slip away. I poked my head into the sanctuary to assess the situation. I needed to start doing more planning and less rushing into things. Impulsiveness had gotten us into this situation in the first place. The last thing I could afford to do now was take an already screwed up situation and make it worse.

After scanning the room to see if it was devoid of other humans, my gaze immediately turned in the direction of the front door. It was too far to see in the gloom, but it was there somewhere, and I needed to find it. When Garrett and I were outside, the locked door had kept us out. Now that I was inside, I hoped like hell it wasn't going to keep me in. I didn't think it would. It was a church door, after all, and the doors of most buildings opened from the inside, even when locked. Even if it had a deadbolt. It was quite possible that I could simply unlock it and walk right on out of the church undetected. Could it really be that simple? Had the genius who'd taken such extreme measures to block my exit through the back door really not thought of doing something more with the front? I didn't know, but I was eager to find out.

My head still throbbed, a reminder of what had happened the last time I left the confines of the mudroom, but it didn't stop me from taking the required steps. Despite the fact that it was too dark inside the sanctuary for anyone to really see me, I chose to stay low and concealed myself behind the pews as I crept along the outer edge of the room.

I was about halfway to the entrance, my heart pounding in my chest, when a sharp bang echoed off the sanctuary's walls, dropping me to all fours. Without a better alternative, I crawled to the nearest pew and slid myself underneath it. Except for the quickened rhythm of my heartbeat in my ears, I found myself completely engulfed in silence. And in that silence, it dawned on me just how quiet it was. The wind was no longer beating up the church, rattling its bones. Apparently, the storm had passed while I was in the coffin. That would easily improve Garrett's chances of finding help – if he had indeed gotten away.

The yellowed pamphlets and mildew-stricken hymnals of a once-thriving church surrounded me while I waited. Waited for someone to come into the room. Waited for the sound to repeat itself. But, no one ever came. All I could think was that maybe an orphaned gust of wind had sent an errant branch against the outside of the clapboard building. It was as good an explanation as any, so I put my trust in that and slowly slid out of my hiding place.

In spite of the militarized voice in my head screaming at me to stay low, I risked a peek over the top of the pew. As far as I could tell, I was still alone in the room. At least it seemed that way. I couldn't see very well in the dark, but my ears were working just fine. And unless someone else was cowering in the void somewhere, I was alone.

From my vantage point, I could just make out the stairway leading up to the loft. Like the rest of the room, the lower stairs were swallowed up by the near darkness. But, as they rose up toward the second story, each individual step grew increasingly more visible due to a faint light now coming from the loft. Even though Garrett and I had found candles burning in the classroom, I felt like the rules had probably changed since Garrett and I had been discovered snooping around. Lights and candles would surely only be used as necessities now, if for no other reason than to make it harder for us to maneuver around and escape in the unfamiliar pitch black. So if a light was on in the loft, I was willing to bet that it was only because someone was up there. As far as who it could be, I had no clue. It could have been either the daughter or the father. But, really, for all I knew, there were other people in the church that I wasn't even aware of. Good or bad, I didn't want to find out.

And with that cautionary thought in mind, I continued toward the front doors with only one goal in mind. Getting the hell out.

Bone **31** White

I was only a couple of steps from it when the front door came into view, and my heart dropped into my stomach. A large, shiny padlock secured massive steel chains that snaked in and out of the door handles. I took the last couple of steps with my eyes closed, silently cursing the bastard for being one step ahead of me. Again.

"Fuck," I whispered, giving at least some voice to my frustration. It was all I could risk, but it was something.

Betting against hope and my own eyesight, I flipped the lever on the door lock and gripped both handles in my hands. With a push, the doors opened slightly, before abruptly clanking to a stop as the steel chain tightened. A mere inch of the outside world peeked through the gap, and a cool breeze hit my face. It was like water to a man lost in the desert. With my eyes closed and forehead pressed firmly against the gap in the doors, I breathed in the damp air like it had been years.

I lived in that moment as long as I dared. The breeze. The pattering of steady rain dancing on the overhang covering the stoop. It was music to my ears after the silent hours inside the church, inside my prison. Still, it was only a taste, and not nearly enough to satisfy my hunger. The carrot that fate was dangling in front of me remained out of reach, a cruel joke that was almost too much to bear. For the first time since the whole ordeal started, a part of me broke free from the rest and resigned itself to its fate. There was no way out. I would die here or be tortured or whatever else might be in the man's plans. My bones were his.

I reluctantly pulled the doors closed until I heard the soft click of the bolt re-engaging. I wanted to stay there longer, breathing in the fresh air that the inside of the building so desperately lacked. I wanted to fill my lungs, at least, with some measure of freedom. But, losing myself in an unattainable mirage wasn't going to get me out of here. Despite my broken heart's resignation, I needed to keep moving. I needed to find a way out.

Yeah, good luck with that, buddy.

With my back against the doors, I surveyed the church's interior contemplating my next move. With an occasional glance loft-ward, I searched the depths of the sanctuary, but saw little more than the vague edges of shapes. *Screw it.* I pulled out my cell phone and flipped it open. It wouldn't matter if I had any battery life later if I never even got out of here in the first place. This time, I didn't even bother checking for a signal. I could only handle so much disappointment at one time, and I was already full to capacity.

Risking detection yet again, I swept the phone's light back and forth across the room in search of something I'd missed. Another exit. Another room. A forgotten gun cabinet stocked with fully-loaded shotguns to blast my way out, a leftover urge from my short-lived fantasy of violence.

No gun cabinet appeared, but something off to my left did catch my eye. A compact alcove had been built into the front corner of the sanctuary. With equal parts optimism and plain old curiosity, I leaned forward and pushed myself away from the front doors. Taking my steps carefully, I walked over to investigate closer. The wall that faced me had hooks mounted to it, obviously for winter coats, rain jackets and things like that. The hooks themselves were naked, tarnished with age and relatively uninteresting. What I did find intriguing, however, was what I discovered on the narrow wall jutting out from the one with the hooks.

A wood-paneled door, short and narrow like the ones in a camper, stood part-way open. I took a deep breath and angled my cell phone directly at it. Its dingy white paint was rubbed bare around the heavily tarnished brass knob. I peered through the eight-inch opening and found nothing except a deeper tone of black. That is, until I thrust my phone into the space. The bluish light revealed a set of wooden stairs leading down into nothingness. It was the doorway to a cellar of some sort. Some place even darker than the sanctuary, that was for sure.

I wished I had a coin on me. In movies, whenever they couldn't see down to the bottom of a well or deep hole, they tossed a coin or something into it to see how far down it went. But then, maybe I should be glad I didn't have a coin. It meant one less decision I'd have to make. Besides, I was pretty sure it wouldn't tell me what I really wanted to know. It wouldn't tell me whether there was a way out down there.

Garrett could be down there.

The thought entered my mind like a flash of blinding truth. Garret *could* be down there, trapped like I'd been earlier. Or, maybe he was fine, but down there searching for another way out as well. As the possibilities ran through my mind, only one thing was certain. The open door stood there like an invitation, practically calling my name. Unfortunately, I was generally a good listener.

Besides, I didn't know what else to do at that point.

Pulling the needle-nosed pliers out of my shorts pocket, I gripped the make-shift weapon in my fist like a knife. With a deep exhale through pursed lips and a soft creaking sound, I accepted the door's invitation.

Bone 32 White

Cavernous. That's how I would describe the emptiness beyond the doorway. Pitch black and hollow. Where the steps would lead me, I still had no idea. The bottom was submersed in a sea of uncertainty as dense and deep as the darkness. The light from my cell only reached so far.

I stepped down onto the first step, then the second, so that I could pull the door closed behind me. But, not all the way. I wasn't sure why, but I didn't want to be completely sealed off from the upstairs. Just in case. I guess in the back of my mind, I was afraid that door, like all the others, would be sealed shut when I came back.

I felt along the cool wall for a light switch, hoping to remove the uncertainty of what lay below. Part of me was afraid of what it would reveal, but every move I made at this point had the potential to blow up in my face. Still, I couldn't just hang out and wait for whatever was going to happen. Besides, if anyone were down there, the light would already be on. Switching on a light packed less danger than tripping over whatever could be ahead of me.

When my fingers finally found the switch, the bottom half of the stairs lit up in a pale yellow, forcing the darkness back into the shadows. The greenish concrete floor, grimy, cracked and uneven, held no promise. The part of me that felt coming down here was a bad idea started clearing its throat for the "I Told You So" speech.

I took the stairs one at a time, pausing after each one to listen for any telltale signs that I might soon have company. But I heard nothing, at all. Not from below, or anywhere else in the church, for that matter. Even my tennis shoes made no sound as I gingerly took each step. I studied my feet as they reached the next tread, puzzled that the boards didn't even creak. Strange for a building this old, but at least I didn't have to worry about accidentally alerting someone to where I was.

Halfway down and the stench hit me square in the gut. A sickening mix of rot, moldy sewage and overlooked dampness. It greeted me like a boisterous uncle, hugging too hard after busting your balls about your father having raised a girl. Acidic bile began rising up in the back of my throat, and I feverishly forced it back down. I doubled over, hands on my knees, from the pungent punch to the stomach. With the constricting stench threatening to take my breath away completely, it took every ounce of intestinal fortitude to keep from heading straight back up the steps. The one thing that stopped me was the knowledge that the way out of this church wasn't up there.

I stood bent over, unable to move, my mind traveling back to a day many summers ago when I learned how to gut a fish. We weren't much older than ten, maybe eleven, when Garrett and I hauled a whole cooler full of blue cats out of the Seneca Park pond. According to the posted signs, we were supposed to release the fish back into the water. But, we were either too young to know better or too excited to give a damn, because we took the whole mess of them back to Garrett's house. There, on his back patio, I got lessons in gutting fish, applying Band-Aids and stomaching foul smells. When Garrett took that first dead fish in hand, slit it right up the middle and all the gore fell out, the smell more than the sight of it got to me. I didn't think I could do it. But, Garrett kept telling me that I'd get used to the smell, and by the time he'd gutted halfway through the bucket, I was right beside him, knife in hand, slitting catfish bellies myself.

This time was no different. After a few minutes of watering eyes, calming inner words, and more mouth breathing than any human being should ever have to do, I started getting used to the stench. In another minute, I straightened up and could continue down the stairs.

Thirteen. That's how many steps it took before the rubber soles of my shoes landed on cold, damp concrete. I had never understood it when people said, "I could feel it in my bones." But, now I did. Understood completely. Even through my shoes themselves were still damp, this felt like I wasn't wearing shoes at all. It felt like the moisture from the floor was entering through the pores in my feet, like some microscopic alien invading my body.

Just above the end of the stairs, the lone light bulb hung by only its wires and illuminated the center of a rather large and soulless basement. Emitting little more radiance than a single candle, it was the only light in a very dark, unwelcoming space, and I couldn't see much more now than I could from the top. I searched the walls for another source of light, but came up empty. The walls remained in shadow; every corner presented a mystery. If there was a way out, it was still waiting to be revealed.

With the yellow bulb shrinking behind me, I held up my cell and began my exploration of the basement, my chest thumping like a war drum. Aside from the nauseating stench, it was like any other old basement at first glance. A rusted antique bicycle, like the ones you see old guys riding along the beaches in California, sat along one wall, propped against a heap of brown, paper grocery sacks, each one filled to the top with Styrofoam packing peanuts. The layer of dust on the bike had taken at least a year to accumulate, and I drew my initials on the seat with the tip of my finger. The bicycle looked like it had been abandoned, all the fun in it either used up or simply being denied. Brown cardboard boxes rested beside the bike, their flaps open, revealing wads of bubble wrap and stacks of smaller, white boxes.

Somewhere in the darkness, a faint dripping sound piqued my interest. I hadn't heard it at first, I'd been so jacked up on adrenalin, but now I could pinpoint the slow, subtle drip coming from farther back in the basement. I told myself that with the way it had been coming down outside, a basement like this was bound to have at least one drip, if not more. Hell, I was surprised the rainwater wasn't flowing right through the walls.

I turned to investigate further, but jerked to a halt when a rustling sound came from one of the grocery sacks. My breath hitched in my throat and I acted on my initial reaction, which was to take a step backward. Once I'd recovered, curiosity got the better of me and I leaned back in to get a closer look. With one hand, I scanned my cell over the stack of crumpled bags. My other hand raised the needle-nosed pliers, gripping them within my assuredly white knuckles. Coming across a mouse wouldn't be unusual in a basement like this, especially out here in the country.

I raised the pliers up to my shoulder, ready to stab at whatever I needed. As the pale light of the cell honed in on the spot in question, two small eyes stared from the sheer black space between two of the bags. The color of pale emeralds, they just stared at me, unblinking, unafraid. The eyes were too large, spaced too far apart to be a mouse. A shiver rattled my shoulders before working its way up the back of my neck. Whatever it was, the animal was a lot bigger than a mouse.

As I pulled back, the creature saw its opportunity and leapt. A mangy blur of black and gray fur sprang from the bags straight at me. It hit my chest and scaled my left shoulder, showering me with white Styrofoam peanuts. My right hand instinctively cut through the air and clipped the prowler with the pliers as it sailed past. The screech of pain identified it as a cat. First disappearing into the immediate darkness, the frightened animal eventually emerged into the light at the foot of the stairs. I caught my breath while watching the cat pad up the wooden steps, its tail curled awkwardly behind it.

Gathering my scattered composure, I inspected the pliers. They were spattered with a bit of blood. There were only a few drops, but what the makeshift weapon lacked in carnage, it more than made up for in hair. A large clump of grey cat hair was matted between the grooved blades. "Ugh," I whispered to myself and wiped the pliers on one of the paper sacks.

Behold, the mighty pussy hunter.

I could hear Garrett's voice in my head and I found myself chuckling at it. If he had been here, he'd have never let me live down clipping off the end of a cat's tail with a pair of fishing pliers just because it jumped out and scared me. I could imagine him bringing it up twenty years from now over beers at my kid's graduation. *Hey, remember that time we were in that old church and that cat scared the bejesus out of you, so you clipped off its tail with a pair of pliers? Remember?* The ridicule would last a lifetime.

But the smile faded with the scenario. Garrett wasn't here. I was alone and had never felt its weight so heavily.

Bone 33 White

I stood with hands on my hips, giving Garrett's voice time to fade. Alone wasn't something I was traditionally good at, and if nothing else, this experience was proving that. I leaned on Garrett too heavily, letting his knack for always knowing what to do take the lead, while being too easily content to take the back seat. All to my detriment. Ridicule or not, I needed him here.

Out of sheer reflex, I raised my cell phone to call him, something I was all too familiar doing. But it wasn't going to work this time. That damned white "X" glowed at the top of the shattered screen. I wouldn't be calling Garrett, or anyone else, from down here. I wasn't completely surprised since I hadn't had service up top, but I squinted at the screen anyway, like I could will it to change. It didn't, but that wasn't what left me deflated seconds later. The battery life indicator showed only nineteen percent.

Shit!

Soon I'd have no more light. Soon I would no longer have the ability to call for help, even after I'd escaped this hellhole. I looked around and shoved the pliers into my back pocket before maiming any other domestic animals. There was nothing to do now but keep searching the basement for cellar steps or a window. Anything that would lead me out of here.

But before turning away, the stacks of boxes caught my eye again, their tidiness a contrast to the filth of their surroundings. They looked like some sort of shipping boxes. I stepped closer and, in fact, a few bore labels, all of them to overseas locations. Uzbekistan, Brazil, Romania. Not from these places, but to them. What was being so carefully shipped from this disgusting place?

A handful of smaller, white cartons lay on a bed of bubble wrap stuffed into the closest box, so I pulled it out. The carton was light and a shake told me it was empty. I opened its tucked flap anyway just to make sure. Apparently, this shipment wasn't ready to go yet. I pushed aside the flap of a more promising box beside it. The white carton in this one was carefully nestled. I picked it up. It was light, but definitely held something. What, I didn't know, and wasn't completely sure I wanted to.

I started to place the white carton back into its bubble wrapped nest, but a shift in the weight inside it elevated my curiosity and I couldn't let it go. With a glance over my shoulder to make sure no one was silently sneaking up on me, my fingers pried open the top. I shook a makeshift tube of plastic wrap into the palm of my hand. A few inches long and less than an inch wide, I couldn't for the life of me tell what was inside. It looked like a stick of chalk, making the idea of writing a note to whoever would receive this package seem like a good backup plan. Plans were good. But backup plans were smart. I picked at the tiny bundle until an end came loose, then unrolled the plastic.

The object that fell into my palm was white, but it wasn't chalk. It was some carnival toy, shaped like –

A skeleton's finger.

I jumped back, throwing the stark white bones at the shipping box they'd come out of. A shout escaped my throat as I did, or at least I hoped it was a shout. What rang in my ears was more like a child's frightened shriek.

Bones. The harvest.

The girl had said it herself. Her father harvested bones. My stomach shook as I stared at the stacks of boxes, waiting to be filled and shipped. Was this the fate of the three girls from my class? Sold off as bones? But who...

It took a stuttering breath to calm my mind. I was letting my imagination run wild, jet fueled by what I agreed now were too many late night horror flicks. There were people who bought bones, sure. I thought of the skeleton hanging in the corner of the biology lab at school. The wired together foot in the doctor's office when he explained which bones were broken after I'd failed to get out of the way of Garrett's bike in fifth grade. People bought bones, so there had to be someone selling them. And that provided a more rational explanation for this evening's events than a sociopathic serial killer and his psychotic daughter simply getting their kicks. I didn't know where legitimate skeletons came from – maybe from alcoholic bums donating their deceased bodies for some quick cash they could spend in the meantime, but I was pretty sure they weren't supposed to come from dug up remains from an abandoned church's graveyard.

His work.

I was fairly certain that harvesting bones, even from a cemetery where they'd never be missed, was illegal, and we'd walked right into *his* illicit operation. The names of the missing girls on the drawings was merely a coincidence, exactly what I thought in the first place, their names pulled from the news by a not-entirely-with-it girl for her imaginary friends.

My rational brain was sold on this explanation. In love with it, in fact. Passionately. It never wanted to part from it. But the rest of me wasn't convinced the relationship was a good one. But then I thought about Garrett. He would accept that explanation and give us both a good natured ribbing for ever thinking anything else. I needed to get a grip and move on. Either that or I would drive myself crazy.

A tall set of wooden shelves lined an adjacent wall where rows of dusty glass jars took up space. Some jars were empty, while others were filled with the usual assortment of nails, screws and various odds and ends. Similar to the jars in my dad's garage, there were probably twenty-year-old artifacts inside that were being held onto in case maybe, just maybe, they'd be needed someday. Except, for these jars, "someday" never came.

With my head much clearer, and with the exception of the illegal bones stolen from the old graves, the basement was proving to be pretty run of the mill. It was time to stop investigating every little thing I saw and find a way out. Once I got away, I would point the cops in this direction where they could come and investigate to their hearts' content.

An old workbench that looked equally unthreatening and comfortable in its surroundings angled from the foot of the stairs. The only thing that stood out about it was its sheer size. It was huge and looked so solid, it had to have been built here rather than carried down. I couldn't be sure of the length, because the bench stretched along the better part of the back wall until disappearing into the shadows. Hell, you could probably take a small car to it and the car would be the one to lose. If there was a window anywhere along the wall, the bench would make it much easier to reach. My fingers were crossed.

A dozen white papier-mâché containers, about the size of Chinese takeout boxes, were stacked neatly on this end of the workbench. Small holes pocked their lids and the word "live" was stamped on their side like the containers our fishing worms came in. I wondered if the guy was a fisherman. Although the dull ache on the back of my head reminded me he wasn't someone I'd be trading fish stories with anytime soon.

A large rusted vise, that looked like it may have been painted grey at one time, was mounted to the front of the workbench, just beside the bait boxes. Thick, white grease covered the screw and it came off easily on my finger. Fresh, I'd say, wiping the oily substance across my shorts.

It's his work.

A shudder ran through me at the thought of someone working here, taking apart decomposed, hundred-year-old corpses in an effort to claim their bones. Hammering the idea home, beside the vise sat a pair of gloves and what looked to be a lawn mower blade with thick, shredded rags wrapped around one end. Both items were covered in reddish-brown stains. An eerie feeling crept over me as I stood there with my mouth hanging open wide enough to catch flies. I had seen enough crime shows on television to know what dried blood looked like. But, this was not television, and this was not one-hundred-year-old blood. Was I mistaking dirt and mud for blood now? I very consciously reached my hand around to make sure the pliers were ready and waiting in my back pocket. Feeling their smooth rubber handles comforted me, although I would have gladly traded them for a big knife at that point. Or that loaded shotgun I was hoping to find earlier.

When I was finally able to pull my attention away from the gloves and scan my cell farther down the workbench, the stained work gloves became insignificant. Everything I'd seen in the church up to that point was forgotten. On top of the workbench, body parts, thrown haphazardly in a pile, were the centerpiece of a visceral and nauseating mess.

Bone and flesh.

Flesh and bone.

And blood. So much blood. Thick and glistening, it seeped into the wood of the workbench's surface, painting it an angry red. Blood so plentiful, it hadn't yet had a chance to dry, and was finding its way onto the floor. The puddle was the size of a trash can lid. A hot ball of lead formed in the pit of my stomach, and I would have thrown it up if it hadn't been lodged in there so tight. It wasn't rainwater I'd heard dripping from the moment I entered the basement. And these weren't hundred-year-old body parts. They were fresh.

He always uses girls.

My legs started to tremble, and I took an involuntary step back, unable to take my eyes off of the selection of body parts. They were piled on the bench like a blood-drenched, disassembled mannequin without its clothes. Then I remembered the piles of clothing in the coffin and the maroon NPHS cheerleading t-shirt the girl had been wearing. They weren't from the dead, or at least, not the long dead. A cold shiver ran the length of my body again, like someone had just walked across my grave. I fought back the vomit rising up. Only this time it came up farther than it had before, and vile stomach acid burned the back of my throat. My face grew flush and sweat broke out on my forehead.

Sometimes, it turns out the calm, rational answer isn't the right one, and those seeping body parts screamed this was one of those times. I needed to get the hell out. This man was no mere dealer in a morbid commodity. He was a madman. And a murderer, and the longer I stayed, the more likely I was to be his next victim.

As I stepped over the pool of red on the floor, I flashed my phone along the rest of the workbench and wall above it. There had to be a window somewhere. But what I found wasn't a way out. A plastic blue tub sat on the very end of the workbench with a sheet of glass across the top like some makeshift terrarium. I couldn't imagine what was in it, and didn't bother with a guess. My feet shuffled in that direction, my chest aching from the abusive pounding it was taking. I pleaded with myself to stop, to turn back. And I wished I would've listened. As the gap between the tub and me narrowed, the sicker to my stomach I felt. When I finally reached it, some force beyond reason guided my eyes down into the depths of the blue plastic.

I immediately cursed myself for doing so.

It was the dome of the off-white skull that came into view first. The bugs came second, crawling in and out of the empty eye sockets like they were doorways. There were hundreds of them. Tiny black and brown beetles were crawling over, around and through what appeared to be a human skull. They milled around, devouring, scavenging just as they were put on the Earth to do. Instantly, I knew my initial assessment had been wrong. There weren't hundreds, there were thousands of them, and I was thankful for the piece of glass separating us.

I found I couldn't turn away from the macabre scene and my attention was rewarded with a vulgar display of nature be nature. One of the beetles stopped at the corner of the jaw and began munching on one of the few bits of remaining flesh. Two more emerged through the gap between the teeth carrying a grey chunk of what might have been brain matter.

A whimper came from over my shoulder, the sound of pure and utter despair, and it took me a moment to realize it hadn't come from me. Once I was sure it hadn't, my heart seized in my chest and the whimper became the only thing that could pull my attention away from the beetles' buffet of human tissue. I spun around and raised my cell phone into the air, trying to shed some light into the abysmal corner from which it had come.

"Jesus." The swear I never used followed, leaving my lips in a whisper, but it was definitely a swear. And if there was ever a need for it, this was it.

Hanging by her wrists from a hook in the ceiling, was a young woman, naked except for a pair of soiled white panties. She was dirty and pale, her skin glistening with sweat despite the cold of the room. She whimpered again, this time louder, and I could see that she was looking right at me. The whites of her eyes caught the light, and I could tell they were open wide.

"Help. Please." The words were murmured more than spoken, and my first instinct was to go to her. My second instinct was to run back up the stairs and jump the fuck out of a window, splinters and shards of glass be damned. Instead, I took a step toward her, still staring. As I got closer, recognition seeped in, leaving me both relieved and terrified.

Becca Lewis was no longer missing.

Bone 34 White

My jacket was still damp from my walk in the lake, but I wrapped it around Becca's naked body before I did anything else. I was fully clothed, with a jacket, and still shivering. I couldn't imagine how cold Becca was or how she was dealing with her time in the basement. But considering the fact that she was shivering while covered in a sheen of sweat, my guess was that she had a fever.

I set my phone, face up, next to the toes of Becca's outstretched feet that barely reached the floor. Holding the jacket around her with one arm, I tried lifting her with the other but, small as Becca was, she was still too heavy for me to lift with just one arm. I couldn't quite get her high enough for the rope around her extended wrists to clear the long tip of the hook. I silently asked Becca's forgiveness, and was about to let the jacket drop in order to use both arms to lift when she spoke.

"Where is he?" The quivering words came so hushed and full of fear, my heart broke in that instant.

"I don't know," I said, after standing up and looking straight into her frightened eyes. "I haven't seen him since he knocked me out and locked me in a coffin. Technically, I never actually saw him, I guess, but we've definitely met."

I'd avoided looking directly at Becca out of a sense of modesty, pretending not to even notice her nakedness in the pale blue light. But, as I spoke to her, I took in her face up close for the first time, and what I saw turned my heartbreak to outrage. Some kind of paint stained the soft, innocent skin of Becca's tear-streaked face. Finger paint, maybe. But, upon closer inspection, it became clear that it was make up. Not only had someone practiced their makeup skills on her, blushing cheeks and all, but whoever it was had done an insanely pathetic job of it. The makeup was preposterous with dark circles painted around her eyes in blue and green, and a grotesquely exaggerated smile in thick red lipstick that nearly stretched from ear to ear. The pink in her cheeks was too profuse, too splotchy and too dark for even the most desperate of men to find attractive.

But that wasn't the intent.

Becca had been turned into a doll.

It had been his daughter. That twisted little bitch, the same one who had hummed a lullaby as I lay locked in a coffin. She'd had her fun with Becca, playing makeup with the frightened girl as she hung by her wrists in this dungeon of horror, just waiting to be cut up and fed to the bugs. My mind immediately went to the lawnmower blade, the bloody gloves and the pile of human limbs on the workbench, and I couldn't imagine the abominations Becca had witnessed down here. The images I conjured alone made me shudder, and I was pretty certain they paled in comparison to the real thing.

Any fear I had was now officially gone, having turned completely to anger. The roller coaster ride continued. Part of me *wanted* to see the man or his screwed up daughter again. I wanted to vent my newfound anger on the both of them. Give an outlet to the violence growing inside me. Beat the shit out of the both of them, cut them into pieces with the lawnmower blade and feed them to the bugs in the blue tub. See how they fuckin' like it.

But, I knew better, and the smarter side of me hoped like hell I never saw either one of them again.

Still holding the jacket around Becca with one arm, I grabbed the pliers from my back pocket and used them to start pulling at the braid of rope snaking in and around her wrists. While I worked, I was cautious not to slip and scrape any skin. The last thing I wanted was to add to Becca's pain.

But the knots were too tight, and this wasn't exactly the job for which the pliers were intended. For this task, I needed something with a knife-edge to cut the fibers. Maybe something serrated, like a handsaw.

My eyes immediately went to the darkened workbench where the very tool I needed sat waiting. Moments ago, I'd wanted to heave at the sight of the lawnmower blade and the bloody rags wrapping it, but now I'd reached that place, down deep, that you don't often see but know exists, and I knew I could do it. I looked at Becca, standing on her tiptoes with her arms stretched high over her head, and realized it wasn't even about whether I could or not. It was something I *had* to do.

I held Becca's gaze for a moment, drawing strength from her pain. Then, as if she was reading my mind, she nodded just slightly.

"Go."

Hesitating only briefly, I told her I'd be right back and picked my cell phone up off the floor. I made my way over to the workbench, sidestepping the bloody slick on the floor. The lawnmower blade sat waiting, its one edge curved slightly upward in an evil grin, like it knew I'd be back. After swallowing a large knot of my own, I took the ragged handle in hand and hurried back over to Becca, but not before shooting a momentary glance to the top of the stairs. All was still quiet. Still dark.

I rushed back to Becca. Seeing her stretched between the floor and the ceiling made me wonder just how long she'd been hanging there. It looked like her arms were about to rip from their sockets at any moment. I shuddered as I imagined her pain, and was encouraged to work fast.

"Hold still," I said, and raised the lawnmower blade up to the rope where it looped over the hook. The rags around the blade were stiff and rough in my hand as I drew the sharpened end back and forth across the rope. There wasn't much room between the tough, fibrous rope and Becca's delicate skin, and I had to stretch up on my toes to angle the blade away from her.

My progress was slow. Too slow. The blade wasn't cutting through the brown rope very well at all. It was almost like it didn't want to. Then it dawned on me, sending a shiver through my entire body. It wasn't a saw, and wasn't used for that purpose. The man didn't use the lawnmower blade to slice through people's limbs. He hacked them off. Like an ax.

"How you doin'?" I asked, trying to get a sense of her condition, and giving my arm a chance to hang by my side for a moment. My shoulder was getting sore, and all the blood draining out of my arm was making my hand tingle. Even as I did it, I felt weak and ashamed considering the fact that Becca's arms had been raised for much longer than the short time mine had been.

"I'm okay," she said, and tried to offer a feeble smile. But, that's all I got. An "okay" and a feeble smile. It didn't tell me much, but I had an imagination, and I knew she was certainly not "okay."

I raised my cell phone to see where I'd been cutting the rope and realized I had barely made a notch, frayed only a few strands. I had to work faster. Positioning the blade back into the notch I'd made, I started running it back and forth with more vigor than I had previously. Putting more pressure, and really getting after it. And it seemed to work. Suddenly, I could hear the fibers shearing as the steel severed each one.

I hung my head down and ignored the ache growing in my shoulder as I worked. I was getting there. My jaw clenched. Back and forth, I sawed at the rope, listening to the wonderful sound of the blade cutting through each braid one by one, and knowing there were fewer to go through with each one severed. But something wasn't right. My hand soon felt wet and the rags around the blade were growing spongy under my grip.

I raised my cell phone a second time and looked up. The horror of what I saw nearly crippled my resolve. Both the rope and the lawnmower blade were slick with blood, shiny, gleaming blood, fresh and bright red. Anxiously, I pulled the blade away and saw that in my frenzy to get through the ropes, I hadn't merely cut Becca, I'd nearly sawed halfway through one of her wrists.

"Holy shit!" I said, then looked at the girl who I had just injured further. The guilt was mounting faster than the words could come out, and I ached like I was the wounded one. "Becca, I'm so sorry."

As I searched her eyes, she looked back at me puzzled.

"What is it?"

"What is it?" I echoed, not believing the question. "I was cutting you. Badly. Why didn't you say something?"

She shook her head, eyes weary. "I didn't feel anything."

And that's when I realized just how bad off she was. I could only stare at her in disbelief, my guilt turning to unforgivable shame as a thin trail of blood dripped down onto her cheek from above. My eyes shot upward, and even without the light from the cellphone, I could see dark lines running the length of her pale arm. The sight was horrific, made more so because I was the one who had caused it.

I looked back into Becca's eyes, not knowing what to say or what to do for her.

"Just get it done," she said, relieving me from having to stare at her sad eyes any longer.

I raised the lawnmower blade back up and, altering the angle so I would miss Becca's skin, began sawing at the rope once more. When the last fiber finally let go, I let out a breath I didn't even realize I'd been holding.

I couldn't support her weight with one arm, and Becca collapsed in a heap on the cement floor. I dropped the lawnmower blade like its very existence disgusted me and knelt beside her. She would probably bruise from the fall, but that was certainly the least of her worries. Or mine. I would have to take care of her wrist before we did anything else. By the way her arm was covered with blood, it was apparent she was losing a lot of it.

After draping the jacket over her shoulders, I worked on the knot that still held the fibrous rope to her wrist. Without the weight of her body holding tension on it, the knot actually proved fairly easy to loosen. Over the years, Garrett had shown me how to tie and untie some of the most difficult of marine knots making this one no match for my skills.

Or Garrett's.

My thoughts went to my friend again, and my stomach churned. For the first time, I found myself skeptical of him having made it out. Between Becca and me, one of us had been tied up and hung from a hook in a cold, damp basement, while the other had been locked in a wooden coffin. So I couldn't even begin to imagine what hell the psycho had inflicted on Garrett. Best-case scenario, Garret had escaped and was busy putting distance between himself and this God-forsaken place.

Worst case? I couldn't think about the worst-case. Too much of it had already come true.

Bone 35 White

The damage to Becca's wrists wasn't limited to what I'd done. Her delicate skin had been rubbed raw long ago. Blood, some red, some a dark brown, smeared her pale skin like mud where the ligature had been. She went to touch one of the wrists, but winced, and my heart broke for her once again. The lowest creature on Earth didn't deserve what she'd been through. With everything she must have witnessed, the pain she'd endured and the humiliation she'd had to tolerate, it was unimaginable. We'd never been "friends," but we knew each other and had classes together over the years. It was enough of a bond to make us more than strangers, enough that I wanted to hold her, protect her, and make sure she had to endure no more.

As I helped her slip her hands into the sleeves of my jacket, I saw her wince again. She was moving so gingerly, it was obvious she was in a lot of pain, and I felt terrible for adding to it. In addition to the rope burns and deep laceration on her wrist, the muscles in her arms and shoulders were probably screaming in an agony that I myself had never felt.

"Can I see?" I asked.

The grimace that came over her painted face made me feel bad for even asking. But, after only a moment and without further coaxing, she nodded and allowed me to gently roll up the sleeve. By the light of my cell, I played doctor and inspected the wound I'd caused. Despite the amount of blood that was still seeping from it, the cut itself didn't appear to be as deep as I thought it would be, given how much it had bled.

"I can fix this," I said, but wasn't sure who I was trying to reassure more.

I grabbed the lawnmower blade and began unraveling the strips of filthy rag from the end. But, after recognizing just how dirty and utterly unsanitary they were, dropped them back onto the floor in a pile. I searched my memory for anything I'd seen since coming down to the basement that might work. There was nothing on the workbench that I could remember. Besides, I didn't want to go back over there if I didn't absolutely have to. After eventually coming up empty, I got an idea, something I'd seen on television. Then clutching the bottom of my tee shirt, I pulled it up and over my head.

"Oh, Luke," Becca said, a sly hint of playfulness in her voice. "I had no idea. Very nice."

When I looked up at her in surprise, Becca raised her eyebrows and managed another weak smile, this one showing a trace of her natural spirit through her tears. She looked like she would have even giggled if she'd had the strength. Instead, a cough racked her chest, and the smile faded as she tried desperately to keep quiet.

I smiled back at her, knowing she was only flattering my skinny ass. I wouldn't consider my muscle-barren body to be "very nice," but it made me feel better to see that Becca still had a sense of humor. And a flirtatious one at that. That was definitely a good sign. This experience hadn't robbed her of that.

I tore off the sleeves from my shirt. Then, one by one, ripped them along the seams, leaving me with two narrow, relatively clean strips of cloth. Being as gentle as I possibly could, I carefully placed one of the strips over the cut and continued to wrap it around Becca's wrist until it ran out. I did the same with the second strip of cloth, but this time wrapped it only once before tying it in a double knot. A slight gasp escaped Becca's lips as I pulled the knot tight, but she didn't pull away. As a small bloom of red started to blossom through the grey, cloth tourniquet, I could only shake my head and allow the feelings of guilt to blossom with it. When I looked up and met Becca's eyes in the dim light, she must have seen the concern on my face, because she managed a real smile this time.

"I'll be alright," she said with a nod. "Thank you."

"Don't thank me just yet," I said, helping her get the zipper started on the front of the jacket. "We still need to find a way out of here, and get help."

Her eyes darted toward the far wall, where the bicycle, paper bags and white cartons were.

"There's a small window," she said, hugging herself through a violent shudder. "It's painted over, but I've been able to tell when it's daytime. It's the only way I even know it's there."

"Can we get through it?" I asked, my eyes searching for the window in the darkness. I raised my cell phone into the air and aimed it in that direction, but the light wasn't powerful enough to reach it.

"Maybe," she said. "But, it's pretty high up. Close to the ceil—"

A sound from above froze us, and we huddled together on the cold floor like cave-bound hikers riding out a blizzard. Somewhere upstairs, a door opened and closed. In that brief moment, the sound of steady rain hitting a tin roof could be heard. It was the same sound I'd heard while standing with the front doors open. That gave me a pretty fair idea who was moving around up there, going in and out. I doubted the daughter even had access to the key for the padlock on the chained front door. In fact, I wouldn't be surprised if the lock and chains were in place as much to keep her in as they were to keep others out.

My heart caught in my chest as an image of the coffin entered my mind. I couldn't remember if I had closed the lid or not. If I had, we might be okay, at least until someone went looking inside it. But if I hadn't closed it … well, we'd know soon enough.

"Light," Becca hissed.

I looked over, reminding her with my eyes not to speak out loud, not with someone so close by. Her eyes shifted toward the bare, yellow bulb hanging at the foot of the stairs. I nodded my understanding. We couldn't do anything about the coffin lid now, but I had to do something about the light. If anyone looked in the direction of the open basement door, that light would easily give us away and we'd have company for sure. That would definitely be bad given Becca's condition and the lack of escape routes down here. On my own, I might have a chance to run, or even fight my way out. But I had wished to no longer be on my own, and fate had granted that request. Becca's company hadn't improved the situation, however. Instead it put me in an unfamiliar one. I was now in charge, and not only of myself, but both of us. The game had changed.

I left Becca's side and crept over to where the bulb hung down. After a quick glance up the stairs, I reached up to unscrew the bulb. The hot glass seared my fingers, but I kept turning. I couldn't risk climbing the stairs to the switch, nor waste time finding more cloth to insulate my hand. I kept unscrewing the bulb until finally, the light flickered and went out, plunging us into complete darkness.

We waited in silence, barely breathing. I could hear my heart pounding against the walls of my chest as I listened for footsteps or anything that would signal immediate danger.

But nothing else came.

All was quiet inside the church again, and that told me two things. First, that someone had probably just left through the front doors. And second, since there was no way to refasten it from the outside, the chain was undoubtedly off.

But, was it worth the risk? Rolling the dice on entering the church had started this whole mess. Risking the lit room in hopes of finding the missing girls had landed me in a locked coffin. Games of chance weren't working in my favor lately, and I was fairly certain my days of taking risks were over. But then I remembered Becca, could feel her shivering beside me as she hugged herself inside my green jacket, her pale face covered in makeup that may as well have been finger paint. And the anger returned; with it came a realization. Garrett wasn't here to call the shots, and Becca was depending on me. If I was going to get us both out of here alive, then I was going to have to take some risks. Standing there, I was reminded of a saying by T.S. Eliot. If my father had quoted this once during one of his lectures, he'd quoted it a hundred times: "Only those who risk going too far can possibly find out how far one can go."

It was time to find out.

My thoughts returned to the window. I wanted to at least check it out before heading back up the stairs. Maybe gambling on the front door being unlocked wouldn't even be necessary. Putting my hands on Becca's shoulders, I whispered in her ear that I'd be right back. Using only the light from my cell, I crept to the far wall. There, above the boxes of bones waiting to be shipped around the world, was the window that Becca was talking about. Just as she said, it was blackened out like the windows upstairs.

Becca was right about another thing, as well. The window was really up there. I mean, way up there. The window was just below the basement's unusually high ceiling, leaving at least eight feet to the bottom of the opening. We would need something to stand on just to get up to it. And helping Becca through in her state was certainly going to put my upper body strength to the test. I remembered the struggle I'd had just trying to lift her up and off the hook. Maybe if I'd been more of an athlete, or at least hit the weights a little more. I made a silent vow to reacquaint myself with the gym after I got through this ordeal.

Becca cleared her throat as quietly as she possibly could, while still getting my attention. Like a good field operative, she waited until I had slinked back over to her before speaking. She'd moved a couple feet to lean against the cold wall for support. In the blue light from the phone, she didn't look quite stable, but she seemed measurably stronger than when I'd unscrewed the light. It was a start.

"Maybe they've left," she whispered.

"I know. I was looking into all of our options, but –"

"The window –"

I shook my head, even though she couldn't see it. "It's too high," I told her. "Even if I could climb up to it and pull myself through…" I let the rest hang there, knowing in the silence that she understood. This was my downfall as a hero. I was too weak.

"Luke?" There was a sadness in the way she spoke my name, and I hoped to never hear it said that way again. "We're going to die here, aren't we?"

My heart splintered at her words, but as it did, it only hardened my resolve. "No," I told her, in a confident voice, "we're not. I have a plan to get us out."

Bone 36 White

It was a bad idea, going back up the stairs, but it was our best option. Our only option if I was going to get Becca out, and not just me. Still, with a window to the outside within my reach, it seemed insane to be taking her up into the heart of the church. Becca stood beside me in silence, waiting for me to make a move.

I could venture out on my own and get help, but it could take hours, and Becca might not survive that long. The hacked remains of whoever's body lay on the workbench told me that much. I couldn't let that happen to Becca. I would like to think I couldn't let it happen to anyone, beautiful girl or not. Most guys have that chink in their armor. It was just something in our DNA, and Becca Lewis definitely fit the beautiful girl description. Even with her matted hair and sunken eyes, an inner beauty still shone through and I was damned if I was going to let anything tarnish that.

"Well," I said, breaking the silence, "if we're gonna do this, let's do it now before he comes back."

Becca put her hand on my shoulder and, with my arm around her waist, we gingerly shuffled our way to the bottom of the stairs, where we took a moment to listen. There still weren't any signs of life from above. The only sounds I could hear were my heavy breathing and the beating of a heart. Whose heart, I wasn't sure. Was it possible that our hearts were beating in unison? Had the stressful, life-threatening situation actually connected us that much?

I dismissed these delirious thoughts, setting them aside for a later date. When we were home safe, there would be plenty of time for them. Now, I needed to focus on my knightly duties. Still, as we crushed together to mount the first step, our arms wrapped around each other, I couldn't help but wonder what our relationship would be like once we had gotten back to our dull lives in New Paris. After all this, would we then consider ourselves friends? Or, would there be something even more behind her smile as we passed each other in the hallways at school?

Obviously, the stress of the situation was getting to me, and I had to shake my head in order to clear it of the craziness. Given the last couple of hours, I think my mind was simply trying to occupy itself with happier thoughts. But first things first.

I unwrapped my arm from around Becca's waist and placed my hand on the small of her back, urging her to go first. Climbing the stairs would go faster in single file, and I wanted to be there to support her if her legs faltered.

One at a time, we took the wooden steps. Her strength was slowly returning and her barefoot steps were proving steadier than I would have thought. To watch her climb the stairs, you'd never know she'd just spent time tied up in a killer's basement. Either she was recovering remarkably quickly, or she just wanted to get the hell out of there really badly. Probably a combination of both.

Four...

Five...

We cautiously ascended the steps toward the narrow doorway, even though we didn't know what awaited us on the other side. It somehow didn't matter. The prospect of being only steps away from freedom propelled us on. Like a comforting beacon, deliverance drew us onward, steering us toward safety like we were a ship that had been lost in a storm.

Eight...

Nine...

My heart beat harder and faster with each step. I'd counted thirteen of them on my way down. We were almost there.

Ten...

Eleven...

Becca's back went rigid under my hand and a faint light burst forth from the alcove above. Or maybe it happened the other way around, I couldn't be sure. My head snapped up to see a hulking man standing in the tiny doorway, a featureless profile silhouetted by the light from behind him. I felt his angry eyes boring into me, reducing me to a child caught sneaking out of the house. It was enough to shatter my veil of confidence, releasing more terror than I'd ever felt. The warm prospect of freedom, extinguished by the icy grip of fear.

Becca gasped as the man's bulging arm shot straight out, stopping in front of her face. I flinched at the sound of a wet thud and a sticky mist hitting my cheek. Becca listed toward me, and my mouth dropped in horror. Sticking out of her left eye socket was a long, white bone. It was roughly the size of one of those miniature baseball bats they sell at the ballpark. Only this was no toy. It was a bone. White and cruel.

Covered in red.

Becca's mouth had frozen in mid-scream, and she started to collapse on the steps. Started to, but couldn't. The man held her suspended by the bone sticking out of her skull, held it like some macabre handle. The feat of strength, for me, added yet another layer of fear.

With the same swiftness he'd shown ramming the bone into Becca's skull, the man's other arm swung around like a windmill. With a flash of silver, time slowed to a crawl. Despite the dim light, I could see the tool clearly. A curved blade. I'd seen it before. Not this one, but one like it, in Mr. Singh's knife collection. The bolo knife had intrigued me the moment Cricket showed it to me. The curve of the blade sloped in the wrong direction for it to be aerodynamic, curving away from the person instead of toward them. But, as I'd seen on the internet, the Filipino tool, while designed that way to cut through vegetation, was also highly effective in the slaughtering of pigs. The images from the slaughterhouse videos ran through my mind as the breeze from the man's blade brushed my face. The blood of the pigs, their squealing, were but distant echoes. The reality wasn't like that at all.

The bolo's blade buried itself in the side of Becca's neck, but it didn't stop there. The brawn in the man's forearm rippled as the blade continued through muscle and bone like it was cutting nothing more than cake. Becca's head separated from her body, coming off clean like a dandelion in the hands of a giggly child. The rest of Becca fell against my arm, too limp for me to keep upright. She crumpled in a heap at my feet, and I knew even before her body hit the steps, that there would be no more passing glances in the school hallways.

Becca was long gone.

And all I could do was stand there, frozen with fear and the utter shock of not only what had just happened, but also how quick it had all gone down. Only seconds ago, our spirits were on the upswing, full of hope. We'd been steps away from the end of this nightmare. Now, the nightmare had taken an even darker turn and her blood was both figuratively and literally on my hands. Becca was dead because I'd chosen the stairs as the easy way out. Dead because I wasn't man enough to lift her out the window. Dead because I wasn't as smart or as strong or as gutsy as Garrett. Becca Lewis was dead because she'd relied on me. And in penance for my sins, I was soon to follow.

I sensed it coming more than I saw it. Acting on an overwhelming urge to duck, I did just that as a large arm swung in my direction. I felt its breeze sweep across the top of my hair. I could smell the tang of blood on the metal blade, but I remained intact. I found myself freefalling backward, my feet kicking wildly, but finding nothing but air.

Eleven steps later, I hit the cold, hard concrete, my shoulder absorbing the initial blow. Unbelievable pain rocketed through me, but otherwise, I was still alive. I curled on my side, breathing in the stale, macabre air as the image of Becca's body rewound in my brain. Her head coming off, over and over. Her body collapsing against me, showing me every humble detail of her severed neck. Muscles. Windpipe. Spine.

With the grief over Becca's death already setting in, all I wanted to do was just lie there in the darkness, surrounded by its concealing comfort and close my eyes. Block out the consequences and curl up into a ball until it was all over. That's what I wanted to do, but my stubborn will to survive wouldn't let me.

A shuffling sound made me open my eyes. The man's silhouette still darkened the doorway, but now from the steps. With a not so subtle nudge, his boot sent Becca's head onto the next step where it landed with the thud and spun around. It came to rest with the bone pointing accusingly in my direction, like some sick version of Spin the Bottle. As her good eye stared directly at me, the first tear of guilt formed in the corner of my eye. In the next moment, Becca's voice screamed throughout my head, pardoning me with a single direction.

Get off your ass and run!

Ignoring the lightening-hot pain shooting through my arm, I scrambled to my feet, my thoughts turning to the window.

Bone 37 White

It came from the front of the church, what her mother would have called a "ruckus." A short scream followed by a low rumble. Nothing out of the ordinary really. Especially considering the arrival of their new guests. New guests always meant strange, new sounds in the church. Moans, screams, cries for help. But, something in this commotion sparked her curiosity.

She set her mother's dirty book down on the bed beside her and straightened out her nightgown. She was reading them herself now. The dirty books. One right after the other. Father was encouraging her to. They'd help her "grow up," he'd said. After all, she was the woman of the house now. Father had his work, and she had hers.

Rising to her feet, she scurried over to the open doorway and leaned her head out. She could hear shuffling sounds coming from the front of the church. Slightly muffled, but loud enough to be heard up in the loft. There were always strange sounds in the church when Father was working. Still, there was something about the scream that stuck in her head. Made her wonder. It didn't sound like a boy's scream. The boy in the coffin had a deep voice. Almost as deep as Father's. This was higher pitched, like a girl's. And she knew perfectly well what a girl's scream sounded like. But, the only other girl in the church was Becca. Her new friend. And, she was deep in the bowels of the basement.

Or was she? Was Father bringing her up? Was it Becca's time to be harvested? The thought made her heart beat a little faster than normal. Her hand went to her mouth and she chewed a ragged fingernail that had long ago given up trying to grow.

No, no, no.

Not yet. She didn't want Becca to be harvested yet. There was something different about Becca. She had spent more time with her than the others, and wasn't sure she wanted her harvested. Not that she'd worked up the nerve to ask Father to let Becca stay. To be her permanent plaything, not temporary like the others. A real friend. But, asking for that would let Father know she had disobeyed him. She had gotten too close. She had asked a name, and look what it had led to.

They're just objects.

He was right. He was always right. Still, she wanted this more than anything.

Her eyes narrowed, drawing lines across her brow. Harvesting took place in the basement. Why would Father be bringing Becca upstairs? Had there been a change in plans? She wondered and wondered until once again, her curiosity got the best of her, and she tiptoed barefoot out onto the small landing at the top of the stairs. Then, she continued all the way down the stairs, skipping only the top step.

The lights were on in the sanctuary. She noticed that before she was even halfway down. It was all lit up like she'd never seen it before. It was like her father was expecting more company, welcoming them by leaving on the light.

That couldn't be right. Every measure Father had taken to keep their presence hidden was done specifically to discourage company. Father preached against the presence of others. Had warned about the consequences, and what it might mean for the two of them. They would take her away. For that very reason, he disliked any lights being on at all, had rarely used them. The bright lights now made her wonder even more.

From the bottom of the stairs, the second thing she noticed was the old, dirty coffin sitting on the stage. Its lid now stood upright. Open. The coffin empty. Her mind raced, and somewhere down deep, in that place where her most secret desires resided, she smiled.

It was harvest time.

Bone 38 White

The squat and camouflaged window taunted me from its heights. I needed something to climb onto just to reach it, and in the little time I had, I realized I had just that: little time. The first direct thud of a boot sounded on a wooden step. Then another. And just that quickly, I was already out of time. With Becca's body having been cast aside, the bastard was already on his way down the stairs.

I looked back up at the window and knew it would have to wait. That fractional part of me wanting a confrontation was going to get its wish. I needed to get my hands on a weapon of some sort. My mind immediately went to the lawnmower blade and the needle nose pliers. What had I done with them? Checking my pockets, I remembered laying them both on the floor once Becca was free. My heart sank.

Idiot!

They were only about fifteen feet away, but may as well have been a mile. Between them and me was the bottom of the stairs, and on the stairs, caught only in the faint light cast down from the church's alcove, I saw legs. Legs clad in soiled denim that ended at blackened work boots, moving purposefully in my direction. I would never make it.

Though the man was moving confidently slowly, like he was the one who had seen too many horror movies and knew just how to act, I still needed to think fast. I had to find something close. Something I could just grab. I searched nearby, but only came up with the ten-speed bicycle and bag after bag filled with Styrofoam peanuts, neither of which gave me much confidence in terms of a weapon. After all, this wasn't a Three Stooges movie. Having quickly dismissed nearly everything around me, my thoughts turned to the only other thing within reach.

The stack of limbs on the workbench. And beyond them, the beetle-covered skull.

I had no time to debate the morality of the thoughts going through my mind. The tone of the approaching steps changed from rubber on wood, to concrete. I took three lunging strides, putting myself right in front of the workbench, a foot from the pile of limbs and nearly side by side with the man. The lack of light was actually working in my favor. We were standing so close, I could smell the sourness of his breath, but he didn't know I was there.

The soft scratching of metal against metal came from the ceiling above. I looked up, zeroing in on its source just in time to be blinded as the light bulb blazed to life between the man's thick fingers. If he was shocked to see me standing beside him, he didn't show it. Instead, his arms shot out without hesitation, grabbing me by the neck like he knew I had been there all along.

White pinpricks joined the spots in my vision left by the light bulb. I fought to see through them, as my arms flailed. Through blind luck, I knocked aside the thin piece of glass from the blue tub. As I struggled through a lack of both vision and breath, my hand dove into the container, and I snatched up the skull by its eyeholes. I swung it, bugs and all, with all my might. The sturdy skull made contact upside the man's temple with a sickening thump and a bone-splintering crack. The skull shattered on impact, leaving only a few shards of facial bone cradled in my fist, and the big bastard dazed and collapsed on the floor in a pool of vermilion blood that wasn't his own.

Bone 39 White

I leaned the dusty bicycle against the concrete wall beneath the window. To say that I was completely trusting of its sturdiness would be a lie, but it was going to have to do. Sure, a ladder or even my grandmother's step stool would have been ideal, but my options were limited. And so was my time. The man was down, but not out. He was murmuring. Even worse, frenzied footsteps thundered across the floor upstairs. We were about to have company. Chances are, it was just the man's daughter and while I was pretty sure I could take her, but there was no telling if she would have a weapon. I didn't want another confrontation. The last one had been too close for comfort, and I had been lucky. Becca hadn't. I wasn't feeling confident in my luck enough to push it again.

The bike wobbled beneath me as I stood on one of the pedals and hoisted my other foot up onto the crossbar. With my hands on the wall, I steadied myself and the bicycle, testing its stability before joining the one foot on the crossbar with the other. I prayed it would hold. Supporting all my weight, the bicycle threatened to buckle or to slide out and away from the wall. Luckily, it did neither. The cracked and deflated rubber tires gripped the floor, locking the bike in place.

The window was eye level now, and I could hear a light rain tapped on the glass. Through the layer of black paint, a faint glow was slightly visible. I assumed it was the floodlight above the tool shed, reaching out to me from the night, and I yearned to reach back. Like a proverbial carrot, freedom dangled its light in front of me. With escape so close, my mind went to Garrett.

Where the hell are you? Last chance to come with me, buddy!

Behind me, the murmurs grew quieter, became almost inaudible, before ultimately stopping altogether. I didn't want to look, but I knew I had to. I didn't like what I saw. The man was up on one knee. He had his hand against his head and was shaking the cobwebs free.

I turned back and fumbled with the antique latch. Rust and corrosion teamed up against me to hold it firmly in place. This window hadn't been opened in years. I pushed hard on the latch with the palm of my hand, but it still didn't budge.

Footsteps pounded down the stairs, sending my already elevated heart rate through the roof. I didn't turn to look this time. I didn't have to. Instead, I stopped pushing on the latch with my palm, began using it as a hammer, pounding away at the metal latch handle. Sharp pains cut into my hand, shooting up my arm with each and every blow. Small cries escaped my lips each time, and soon my trembling arm begged me to stop. But, this was my only way out now. It was too late to do anything else.

"Come on, dammit!"

I expected to be grabbed by the back of my shirt and pulled off the bicycle any moment. I imagined myself being thrown onto the cold, hard cement floor, much the same way

I'd been thrown into the coffin earlier. My heart bludgeoned my chest, threatening to burst with every progressive beat. And for the first time since everything went south, tears blurred my vision, but still I pounded on the latch handle. Pounded and cried. From pain. From crippling grief. From the knowledge that, if this didn't work, I was certainly dead.

I was about to give in and use my elbow to bust out the glass when the latch slid out of its seat. Since I wouldn't have had time to clear out all of the broken shards of glass, I wasn't looking forward to the fillet job they would have done on my body. But that was no longer an issue. A small wave of relief came over me.

Clean and shiny metal slowly appeared on the latch as it slid out from the rusted metal casing. With one final slam of my throbbing palm, it came completely free. Knowing it would take all I had, I grabbed the latch with both hands and yanked the window open, giving it no other choice. A loud tearing sound filled the room as the thick layer of paint separated itself. The momentum nearly toppled me from the bicycle, but I hung onto the window like a trapeze bar as it swung inward and was able to keep myself from falling.

It was the sound of steady rainfall and the cool air against my face that welcomed me. Beckoned me. Practically grabbed me by the wrists and started pulling me from the sickening necropolis of death and insanity. The window was short and wide, barely tall enough for me to squeeze through. But, it was enough. The man would be too big to fit, and that knowledge alone was enough to urge me on. I only needed to get through this window and I'd be free. I smiled through the last of the tears.

I grabbed the bottom of the windowsill. It was only when I had a death grip on the sill and was about to hoist myself up, that I risked a peek behind me – and wished I hadn't. The daughter was beside her father, helping him to his feet. She glared at me, her eyes ablaze. If looks could kill, I'd be lying in a heap on the workbench, waiting to be picked clean by bugs. Fury rose up in her throat and burst out as the most God-awful scream, nearly dropping me from my perch. It was a crazed, obsessed scream, sending chills from the base of my skull, down through my entire body.

As the scream faded, my eyes locked onto the man's for the first time. We stared at each other for an eternity, he and I, gauging each other's emotions, sizing up the adversary. His eyes bore a frightening union of anger and desperation. His life depended on catching me. And killing me.

He took his first step in my direction.

My arms and legs worked to raise me into the window frame. Once my feet left the bike, it clattered to the floor behind me, hopefully buying me an extra second or two. Almost immediately, my chest fell sharply against the metal window frame, making me wince. My legs were no longer of use. They blindly kicked the air behind me, as I flopped around like a fish out of water.

The sound of metal hitting the concrete wall clanged beside me, then banged onto the floor. *A knife? Something larger?* I wasn't sure, but something had been thrown at me and I chalked it up to another near miss. With all the strength in my arms, I pulled and wiggled the rest of my body through the window, expecting to be seized by my ankles at any moment. But, it never happened. The bicycle must have done its job.

An overgrown flowerbed surrounded me as I lay face down in the mud. Weeds and vines and flowers, long dead, laid crumpled in the soggy earth beneath me. Cold rain pelted the back of my neck, and my only thought was that it had never felt so good to be caught out in it.

I pulled myself up onto my knees, and peered back through the window. Like some classic cartoon, I expected to see the bad guy shaking his fist, telling me that this wasn't over. The pool of light at the bottom of the stairs illuminated the concrete floor. There were white bone fragments from the skull scattered around bloody boot prints, but otherwise, the basement was empty. The man and his daughter were gone.

PART III

*Yea, though I walk through the valley of the
shadow of death, I will fear no evil.*
- Psalms 23:4

Bone 40 White

With the front of the church to my right, the tool shed with its floodlight to the left, I bolted straight ahead toward the overgrown parking lot and long winding driveway that led Garrett and me into this nightmare in the first place. It seemed like days had gone by. Days since we'd been on the lake in Garrett's boat. Days since we were enjoying the time away from New Paris and its missing girls.

Days since I hadn't felt fear.

The good news, there was one less girl missing now. I'd found Becca Lewis, maybe even the other two amid a jumble of dismembered body parts on the workbench. Unfortunately, there was a whole shit ton of bad news. None of the girls would be going home. They wouldn't be running into their kitchens and wrapping their arms around their mothers' necks, thankful to be home. They wouldn't be in class on Monday morning. They wouldn't even be leaving that church alive.

I wanted to go back and get Becca, to bring her with me. I knew it wasn't possible, but as the falling rain ran off my forehead and into my eyes, I found myself choking back feelings of guilt and despair. Guilt that I had made it out while unable to save Becca like I'd promised. Despair at the knowledge that nothing in the world would ever be whole again. All the wrongs could never be made right. My life would never be the same.

Like a crack of thunder, a sharp bang came from behind me that stopped me in my tracks, my shoes barely getting traction in the half gravel, half mud surface. Without thinking, I turned to see what the noise was. Big mistake.

On the darkened stoop of the church, the front doors were bouncing back from having been thrown open against the church's clapboard siding. In the doorway, silhouetted against the blazing light from inside the church, stood the outline of the massive man, his head working back and forth as his eyes scanned the grounds. My heart sank. It was too soon. He shouldn't have been out there that quickly. As I suspected, the front doors had not been chained. Knowing we'd been so close and yet, Becca was dead because of it, was like a kick in the stomach.

But, there would be plenty of time to grieve later. The way the man cleared the steps in one impressive leap let me know I'd been spotted. I wasn't sure if it said more about his athleticism, or his desperation. As if either of those things wasn't enough to instill fear, he carried something long, curved and shiny in his hand. The bolo knife. Athletic and carrying a weapon. That made two things he had over me. But desperation was on my side was well. I knew what was riding on him catching up to me. I knew what it would cost. Images of how gruesome my death could be urged me to run.

Bone 41 White

I considered joining track last fall for the only reason an un-athletic guy like me would ever consider joining track: because of a girl. Shari Maxwell. The only girl I'd ever met that made me want to try something that was outside of my comfort zone just to get close to her. Then, two weeks before tryouts, Shari found out she was pregnant, our starting tight end mysteriously chose to quit the football team and get a part-time job, and I ended up not joining track after all. Luckily, fate stepped in and saved me from two months of unnecessary athletic misery.

Now, though, I wished I'd joined the team anyway. I probably had twenty years or more on this guy and was leaner by at least fifty pounds. Still, he was gaining fast. Gaining fast and closing the gap between us. I could hear his footsteps splashing on the soggy driveway behind me. And as impossible as it was, I swore I felt him literally breathing down my neck. Obviously, fear was skewing my perception. If he'd actually been that close, he would have cut my legs out from under me by now. It was then I decided that, just like joining a team because of a girl, running straight down the driveway was a piss poor plan.

Ignoring a lifelong phobia, I cut sharply to my right and darted straight into the woods. Straight toward the lake. The dense wilderness and darkness I once feared now embraced me and swallowed me up, but in a good way. If I couldn't outrun the guy, my best chance was to lose him in the trees. Chances were, he knew the area better than me. But, I couldn't worry about that. I just had to put my faith in the notion that, if he couldn't see me, he couldn't catch me. Best case scenario: the woods were thick enough to provide cover, yet not so thick as to impede me from making my way through.

As soon as I felt I was out of sight, I veered left and ran parallel with the driveway for another twenty yards or so. At least I ran when I wasn't ducking and weaving. I'd definitely gotten my wish. The woods were as thick as black-clad teenagers at a Marilyn Manson concert. The trees themselves were like zombies, constantly reaching out for me, snagging me, carving up my bare arms. I passed a large clump of thorny brush that was overtaking a fallen tree and cut back to the right, toward the lake again. I figured a zigzag route would be better than a straight shot. I'd heard that somewhere, but couldn't remember where.

The footing on the water-logged soil wasn't great, but the layer of pine needles and fallen leaves provided decent traction over the mud, allowing me to navigate the maze of trees and brush with only minor slipping and sliding. Still, the slick soles of my tennis shoes weren't the best option for running through the sloppy landscape. Had I known what I'd be doing, I would have worn my trail shoes, which were made for terrain like this. But, then, let's be honest, had I known what I would be doing, I wouldn't have come on the trip in the first place. I would have spent my Friday night either playing video games with Cricket, or hanging with Claire while she babysat the Kitner twins.

As I slid on my ass over a slimy, moss-covered log, the thought of my friends took me back to a world that seemed so very far away. It was my world, and I hoped like hell I'd get back to it. I didn't want to live in this world any longer, didn't like it. Though, even if I did make it back, I knew I would be taking at least some of this world back with me. Whether I wanted to or not.

With a sky full of rainclouds and treetops to block out any chance of a stray moon ray, the nighttime inside the woods was nearly pitch black, which was both a good and a bad thing. The fact that I couldn't see him, and didn't know where he was, added a little more tension to the situation. But hopefully that meant the bastard couldn't see me, either. And if he couldn't, maybe he'd give up eventually, if he hadn't already. Hopefully, I would soon be left alone within the trees. But, I realized that was a hell of a lot of hoping on my part. Even so, I was at least feeling like I'd made the right decision by running into the woods. Finally, things were starting to go my way.

Bone 42 White

Her father wouldn't be back for awhile. Not without the boy, at least. He was persistent that way. Her mind flashed back to the night her father brought home the second girl. The first one that was still alive. The blonde. It had taken her the entire following day to clean up all the blood. And not all of it was the girl's. Some of it had been her father's. The girl had foolishly fought hard to live, but Father had fought even harder for her not to. He never gave up, and she had been so proud of him.

But, that's how it had to be now. They had to live, and some things had gotten more difficult and more dangerous because of it. When the harvesting of old cemetery bones came to an end and the harvesting of new bones began, Father really stepped up trying to hide the fact that they were living in the church. Not that he'd run out of old bones. Plenty still rested in the gravesites in that old cemetery. But the old bones didn't get as pretty and white as the new ones. That's what Father said. And she had agreed. New bones were much prettier. They also brought more money, so that settled it, and it suited her just fine. She didn't like him bringing caskets into the church. Something about their oldness creeped her out.

She paced the well-worn floor of the church's entryway, wondering many things. She wondered if she should turn off the lights. If it even mattered anymore. More importantly, she wondered how much longer it was going to take. It was late, and she was tired. She wanted to go to sleep. But there was no way she could, not with all this energy running through her. They'd had a lot of excitement for one day, and now she was both exhausted and exhilarated.

She was also angry. Blisteringly mad. The boy had tried to take Becca away, forcing Father to kill her in order to stop them. And she'd liked this one. Becca. She knew what her father had said about the names. Not knowing made it easier. But, this girl had looked very much like her mother, from what she remembered at least. Having Becca to play with and talk to made it seem like her mother was still around. So she'd had to ask the girl's name, and didn't regret it.

But now, Becca was dead. Like her mother, if she was truly honest with herself. And it was all that boy's fault. She didn't know *his* name and was glad for it. Father was right. It did make it easier. She hated the boy for causing this. For having the nerve to come here and cause these problems. Hated him just as much for hurting her father. But, he would pay. Father would catch him and he would pay. Of that, she was certain. In her imagination, she played out how it would go down, and the thoughts brought on a smile. Her father was really good at making people dead.

Bone 43 White

Raindrops trickled through the treetops, dripping onto my head as I stood in the mud peering through a rusted chain link fence. Rising eight feet into the air, it cut through the trees, separating me from where I needed to go. I'd nearly run right into it in the darkness. I imagined the metal cutting me into tiny slivers like a French fry press. I wasn't sure if the fence was there to keep people out, or to keep people in. Given everything I'd seen, the reason for the fence could have really gone either way. At this point, it didn't matter. All I knew was that it was not about to keep me in. This wasn't the first time Garrett and I had been caught somewhere we weren't supposed to be. And being chased off someone's property, more often than not, meant scaling a fence or two.

As my old friend entered my mind again, I realized that thoughts of his safety could only be fleeting at this point. I hoped he was somewhere safe, but that's all I could afford him. I was in deep trouble myself, and was finding less and less time in my busy schedule to worry about him. Whatever was to be, would be. Though the thought had crossed my mind that my keeping that psycho occupied could only benefit Garrett. I'd be lying if I said I wasn't hoping my friend would be at the boat waiting for me when I got there, but I wasn't counting on it. If the last couple hours taught me anything, it was that I was alone. No one but me was going to save me.

I reached up, slid my fingers through the metal wires, and after sliding the toes of my tennis shoes into the gaps, hoisted myself off the ground. The toe of my shoe was too wide to go in very far, but it was enough to get some leverage, albeit precariously. I repeated the process, carefully coordinating my hands and feet, until I was almost at the top of the fence. It didn't seem to take nearly as long to scale the fence as it normally would. But, then, I had an incentive this time that I'd never had before. The threat had never been so severe, the consequences so final.

I swung my right leg over the top of the fence, and after a few blind attempts, finally found a place for my foot. It was only when I was swinging my other leg over that I was able to glance back in the direction I'd just come. About twenty yards behind me, a flash of white cut through a shadowy space between the trees. It was immediately followed by the loud snapping of a twig, loud enough even to be heard over the gentle rain falling on leaves. I wasn't sure if it was the man or not. Could have been a deer. I wasn't even sure it was heading in my direction. But, seeing it at that moment was enough to rattle my concentration.

My foot slipped out from under me, bringing the ground up fast. In the fraction of a second I had, I instinctively shot out my hands, grasping at the fence as I careened toward the forest floor. Failing to latch onto anything but air, they skidded down the crisscrossing links, the rusted metal scratching and slicing the skin of my fingers all the way down.

I landed on both feet, but not softly or gracefully. My left ankle buckled under my weight, and a loud pop rang out just as a red-hot pain seared up my leg. I knew the sound I'd heard wasn't the snapping of a stick, but bone. My left leg was bent at an awkward angle just above my ankle. It was broken. There was no doubt. I'd never broken a bone before, and I couldn't have imagined the pain. As it was, it took all I had to keep from wailing like a baby. But as I lay there, broken on a muddy carpet of pine needles and leaves, I gave in and the tears flowed freely. At that point, there was simply no stopping them.

Bone 44 White

She was worried. A feeling she rarely experienced living in her secluded little world. Although she had grown accustomed to it over the past year or so, she knew how secluded it was. And how little. She hadn't forgotten about going to school, the grocery store and a number of other places with her mother. Been a part of the outside world. But, all that was behind her now. Father insisted on doing all of the errand running alone. Getting the groceries and the supplies he needed. Picking up the girls. It was safer for the both of them that way, he said, and she tried to understand. Couldn't argue. He protected and provided for her, and like he always told her, that's all she could ask for. It was his work, and he did it for them. Someday they would have lots of money to travel, to visit far off places. That's what he promised. To live the life of a king and queen. Someday, he told her. Someday.

Now, though, it had been over an hour, and he still wasn't back. She wondered if she should go out and help find the boy. Father had told her to stay behind, though, to ready things for the harvest. But everything Father needed for the harvest – the plastic, the buckets, even the lawnmower blade she'd found tucked in the shadows of the basement – were laid out and waiting. All she could do now was wait. And for her, the waiting was always the hardest part.

She wrung her hands as she paced the floor. Wrung them until they were sore. She couldn't help it. She didn't know what else to do with them. It made her antsy, the waiting. She hated it. Despised just sitting here while her father was out searching. Especially since she'd become the woman of the house. She should help out more. She needed to be more involved. Wanted to do more than just get things ready and clean up after. Had felt that way for awhile now. After all, she was sixteen, if her math was right. But, Father always told her "someday." Always someday. But, she was ready now. Ready to help. Ready to do his work.

When she could stand it no more, she slipped into the faded jeans and maroon sweatshirt Becca had been wearing when she'd arrived and took the stairs from the loft down to the sanctuary. Even though her own stink had recently crept into the material and replaced the floral scent of her friend's perfume, she still liked wearing Becca's hand-me-downs. Still liked being close.

In the mudroom, she slipped on a pair of boots that were three sizes too big and her father's slicker that hung on a hook beside the boarded up back door. The wooden boards that stretched across the door caught her attention. She wasn't surprised to see them. On the contrary, they seemed fitting enough for her to wonder why the door hadn't been boarded up before now. They also reminded her how her father had told her to stay behind and remain in the church. Like always.

But this wouldn't be the first time she'd explored the surrounding woods while he had been away. Only the first time he would be aware of it. There had been more than a few times when he'd made a run into town, leaving her behind, and she had snuck out the back door for an adventure of her own, comfortable in the fact that he would be gone for hours. In fact, she might even know the surrounding area better than he did. Besides, all would be forgiven if she were to find the boy and bring him back. Then Father would know she was ready and things would be different. Perhaps she would even be rewarded. Maybe she would be allowed to do the harvesting this time. Make the boy dead. The thought brought a smile to her lips, a flicker of excitement in her belly, a warmth between her legs.

Atop the narrow ledge above the church's front doors, she knew her father kept a small hatchet hidden "just in case." She reached up and ran her fingers along the length of dusty wood until they finally brushed against cold, sharpened steel. Pulling the small ax down by the handle, she assessed the heft of it and allowed herself a full smile. Then, making sure they weren't going to lock behind her, she closed the front doors on her way out.

Bone 45 White

My left foot dragged the mud behind me like a rock tied to a rope. Like dead weight. The pain was excruciating, and it had taken all I had to get off the ground and keep moving. I tried to hop on my good foot, but couldn't keep it up, not to mention I wasn't getting very far. So even though putting weight on it hurt like hell and brought the salty tears all over again, I did it as best I could and eventually, grew numb to the pain. Now, as I walked in the direction I hoped would ultimately lead me to the lake, I carved a shallow, but noticeable trench in the rain soaked leaves and mud. A blind man with a scarf over his eyes could have followed the trail I was leaving, even under the cover of a blackened night.

Above the tops of pines, oak and ash, lightning fractured the sky, followed swiftly by a low rumble of thunder. With the exception of a mild, yet steady rainfall, the skies had been fairly calm since I'd escaped the church and the rumbling sky was the first significant sound I'd heard from the outside world since leaving there. I wasn't sure if this sudden outburst was the start of something new, or just an isolated storm cell passing nearby. My hopes revolved around the latter. As good a shelter as the canopy of trees had been earlier, there had simply been too much rain since then.

The drizzle was finding its way through the treetops, tagging me in the process. A violent shiver took hold of me, starting in my shoulders. My jacket was back at the church, still wrapped around Becca's dead body. My thin, now sleeveless t-shirt was soaked through, and the dark grey cloth clung to me like shrink-wrap. My sopping hair was plastered to my head, and I had to blink back the streams of water running down my face. Rain? Tears? At this point, it could have been either, and I didn't really give a damn which.

I just wanted it to be over. The fear. The torment. I wanted to give up. Throw in the proverbial towel. Drop down onto the soft forest floor and wait for whatever was to happen. Wanted to, but I didn't. I trudged onward, pushing down the forces inside me that threatened to grind what little sanity I had left into dust and cast it into the wind. How long had I even been wandering these woods? An hour? Two? It probably wasn't as long as it felt, but it was still a long fucking time.

I used my bare arms like machetes, hacking my way through the dense brush. The talon-like branches sliced my skin with ease. The occasional rogue limb found my face, slashing it. I was sure a couple of them had drawn blood. I could taste it as it mixed with the rain and ran down into my mouth. Each scrape momentarily took my mind off my shattered ankle. But only momentarily.

Lightning and thunder remained at bay, but the rain had picked up again, pounding everything around me. Its roar came from all directions, disorienting me like a child lost in a crowd. I didn't know if I was going in the right direction. I didn't even know what the right direction was. Should I make my way toward the road? Or should I try and find a house somewhere in this God-forsaken stretch of woods? And if a house, then a phone. Ultimately, my gut told me just to get to the lake, maybe just because it was more familiar. Once there, I would have more options and could figure out a more complete plan.

The latest deluge of rain wasn't entirely a bad thing, however. Occasionally, I would stop walking and tilt my weary head back, open my mouth and let the rain running off the overhead leaves moisten my parched throat. I found it ironic how I could be soaked through to the bone, yet my throat remained dry. I stopped now and then to drink. And when I stopped, I also listened for the man behind me. Listened for a car on an unnoticed, nearby road. Listened for any sign of life among the trees besides just mine and his. But I heard nothing except rain. Generally, not hearing him behind me would be a good thing, though it could be that I wasn't hearing him simply *because* of the rain. And that could be bad.

Very bad.

Mud caked onto the bottoms of my tennis shoes to the point where every step I took, I slid an extra inch or two. Despite the pine needles and leaves, the forest floor was quickly turning into a real mess, and slowing my progress. I used trees for balance whenever I could. At one point, as I tried to gracefully sidestep a giant-sized snake hole, I slipped on the landing and fell, banging my shoulder hard against a tree. I winced from the sudden jolt of pain, but stifled the cry that rose in my throat, not wanting to give away my location. It would have been a cry of frustration as much as pain, and I bore the anger inside just in case I needed to use it later.

As quickly as I could, I scrambled up onto my good foot, pulling on branches and ivy with bloodied hands. I couldn't afford to stop or even slow down. My ankle ached with a pain like I'd never imagined, and with each step it grew worse than before. It would eventually go numb from time to time, and when it did, I couldn't ask for anything more.

A lack of pain due to shock was something I shared with Becca. She'd not felt me cutting her skin as I'd sawed the rope that bound her wrists. And if there was one thing that I was thankful for, it was that there would be no more pain for her. No more fear. I didn't save her, but I'd inadvertently helped end her ordeal.

As the torrent of water continued to fall, I struggled to see anything through the curtain of darkness and towering trees. Still, as if we were somehow connected by this struggle for life and death, I felt the man behind me. I knew he was still there, creeping through the same woods. A hunter stalking his prey. So far, I'd done a good job of ignoring everything I'd ever feared about being in the woods at night. In fact, I hadn't even thought about it. Apparently, imaginary monsters don't mean squat once you've gone up against a real one.

Bone 46 White

She had just started down the driveway, slipping in the mud, when her eye caught the tiny wooden shed behind the church. With the weak floodlight mounted on its side, it looked lonely sitting under the falling rain. Lonely like her. Only the shed still had a friend, and she no longer did.

She found herself torn, knowing full well she shouldn't waste any more time. The boy from the coffin already had a considerable head start, and if her father hadn't caught up to him yet, her chances of catching him were dwindling with every minute she let tick by. If she was going to prove herself to Father, she would have to hurry. But, she also wanted to know. Had to know. Who was the other boy? What had her father done to him? He hadn't had time to harvest the boy, if that was even his plan. And she was pretty sure that it was. What else could be done at this point? Too much had been found out. Too few options remained. Regardless, the boy in the shed was a mystery to her. A mystery begging to be solved. A mystery she was quickly finding herself unable to let go of.

Bone 47 White

Only a couple of more hours of darkness remained, of that I was certain. Soon, the sun would be coming up and this night would be behind me. According to the clock, at least. The dark woods, with shadows deeper than the night itself, would lighten and the shadows themselves would be forced to retreat for another day. Navigating my way toward the lake would be so much easier in the daylight.

But then, I thought, so would tracking me.

The rain was letting up just as exhaustion was setting in. My body was begging me to lie down, to close my eyes for at least a few minutes. But, would it be for only a few minutes? The weariness in my bones and muscles said there was no way I could rest my eyes without completely dozing off. When I finally got the chance to sleep, it would be for a very long time. Days maybe, and now wasn't the best time for that.

But the sun would help. It would keep me awake. I knew that as my plan changed in the half hour since banging my shoulder into the tree. As much as I needed to stay ahead of the game, I was also on the lookout for someplace to hide. Someplace to lay low until the sun lit the sky. The fact was, I should have reached the lake long ago. In addition to being tired, or maybe because of it, I feared I was going around in circles. At any moment, I might stumble upon that chain link fence again. And if that happened...

Yes, daylight would help me stay on course.

Besides, I was just so weak, struggling to put one foot in front of the other. I lacked the energy needed to ignore the pain in my ankle and press on. I hadn't eaten anything since the gas station hot dogs Garrett and I bought on the way to the lake the day before. We'd left the rest of the food back on the boat. Not that I really felt like eating. Hunger and food were tied in the competition for the farthest things from my mind, though it would have been nice to have the fuel. When faced with possible extinction, the will to survive is a powerful force and can push you farther than you would normally have the endurance for. But, without food and rest, your body will inevitably break down and give out at some point. Those action movies where the characters go for days without sleep? Yeah, that's all bullshit, and I was learning it firsthand.

I was just about to collapse, to let the last remaining drop of energy in my body spend itself and cash out, when I saw the crevice in the ground. I almost stumbled into it, actually. It was just a V-shaped depression in the ground, as if the hull of a boat had sat there for ages. The narrow trench followed the slope downhill, growing wider as it went. The sound of running water gurgled from its bottom several feet below. My brain started processing. Like the narrow rivers I'd seen flowing across the churchyard, all this rain had to be going somewhere. And that somewhere was exactly where I wanted to go. My bet was that, if I followed the running water, it would eventually lead me to the lake. I didn't know where on the lake, but it had to be somewhere not too far from the sandy stretch where the boat waited.

Once I hit the shoreline, going left would get me to the boat. With the motor's busted prop, I wasn't sure how I was going to get back to the truck once I'd found the boat. But the truck wasn't necessarily the only option. Just being out on the lake would put me one step closer to safety, creating some much needed distance between me and the man. And who knows? Maybe there would be houses farther down the shore and people who could help.

Finally, I had a plan that was giving me an ounce of confidence. It gave me a direction to follow. The exhaustion I was carrying in my shoulders and neck eased slightly, and I breathed a little easier. Things were looking up. But, first, as much as I hated to take the time, I needed to rest my leg.

Bone 48 White

Disappointment fell heavily on her shoulders when she saw the grey door's latch. It bore a large black lock with the word "Master" stenciled in white. It hadn't been there before. She hadn't known her father to ever lock the shed. But, it wasn't altogether surprising. As much as he had allowed her to see of his operation, there were probably still a lot of aspects of her father's work that she didn't know about. Yet, she reminded herself. She didn't know about them *yet*. But, she would. Very soon.

She took the cold and wet steel box in her hand and gave it a tug. She didn't know why. Just the off chance that it might be unlocked. But it wasn't. The lock was fully engaged, just as she knew it would be. It didn't budge, and she let the lock drop back against the wooden door. The slight thud was barely audible over the nearby rustling leaves.

With the hatchet ready at her side, and the rain still falling steadily down upon her, she leaned in and tried to look through the thin gap between the two doors. The doors were old and hanging crookedly, creating a gap between them just wide enough to be able to see between. But, the inside of the shed was too dark. Too black. She couldn't see a thing, and her shoulders sagged even further.

"Hello," she said, then waited for a response. When none came, she tried a second time, only louder, making sure she was heard over the constant noise surrounding her. "Hey, you. Boy." Still nothing, and her forehead began to wrinkle in on itself. She knew he was still in there. Her father hadn't had time to remove him, and the doors wouldn't be padlocked if he had. There would be nothing to hide, and no reason to keep anyone out. Or keep anyone in.

In a last ditch effort to communicate with the boy in the red jacket, she pounded on the wooden door with the butt end of the hatchet blade. Waited, then pounded again even harder, allowing a little of her frustration out. The doors clattered back and forth against each other, at least as much as the lock would allow. But, still no response came from inside the shed. Her head cast downward, she turned away from the shed and started slopping her way once again toward the driveway. The hatchet, like a relay baton gripped firmly in her hand, swung impatiently at her side, eager to do some work of its own.

Bone 49 White

A bolo knife sliced through my leg, waking me with a jolt. The blade ripped through the skin just above the ankle, and didn't stop there. It severed the muscle. It sliced through the bone. Sprays of thick, black blood erupted from the remaining stump like lava spewing from an awakened volcano, filling the air with a mist, saturating the ground around me. I shot up, instinctively grabbing for the lower part of my leg, frantically searching for what I feared would be gone.

My leg was still there, fully intact, and I breathed a sigh of relief. Once I had a chance to rub my eyes and clear the cobwebs out of my head, I realized it had only been a dream. My elevated heart rate started to back off. My eyes drifted closed again, and I allowed myself to breathe easy.

But, I wasn't celebrating just yet. My leg may have been safe, but I wasn't happy with myself for falling asleep. That sure as shit wasn't the plan, and it would have been a foolish one if it had been. As it was, I was lucky as hell the man hadn't stumbled upon me while I was out. Had I been snoring, sending out alerts like some kind of homing device? Hell if I knew. There wasn't even a way to know how long I'd been out. I wouldn't swear by it, but the woods seemed just a little lighter than what I remembered. Not much, but a little.

With my eyes closed once again, I racked my memory and tried to think back to the last thing I remembered doing before crawling into the trench. I needed to get a sense of how long I'd been out. I remembered trying to make a phone call. My phone had signal. Only two bars, but that was two more than I'd had all night. I'd hit the retry button to call my mom. My spirits had soared at the ear candy of the phone ringing on the other end. The sweetest sound I'd heard in a long time.

But my joy didn't last. After two rings, the phone went silent. I'd waited a few seconds, and when nothing happened, I'd pulled the phone away from my ear and checked the screen. The words *call connected* spread across the bottom like a destination on a treasure map, only the treasure wasn't there. After saying my mom's name a couple times without response, I'd snapped the phone shut in frustration and tried again. Only this time, there was no ringing at all and the words *call failed* flashed in red on the screen. I'd tried a couple of times more, but got the same result each time. Even holding the phone high up in the air hadn't done any good.

After convincing myself that throwing the damn phone deep into the woods wasn't a good idea, I'd regrouped and checked out my surroundings to see where I stood. In the crevice with me were several discarded items like someone had used the trench as their own private garbage dump. A cinder block, two sections of chain link fence that looked very familiar, several masses of tangled fishing line, some empty beer cans, an old camouflaged baseball cap and a worn out car tire. Unless I was cornered and wanted to throw beer cans at the guy, there was nothing of real use. Although the tire proved to be a much softer footrest for my ankle than the cinder block. For that I was appreciative.

Cold, soaked to the bone, and now covered in mud from climbing down into the trench, I grabbed onto a thick tree root that protruded from the crevice wall just above my head. Using it for leverage, I hoisted myself up just enough to see out over the edge. My first instinct had been correct. It was lighter out than when I'd first crawled in. Not yet dawn, but that half hour or so just before. If they had a name for this time of day, I didn't know what it was. But, I was thankful for it. I could see farther down the crevice and had a better idea of where it led. I could make out profiles of trees from a distance that had been only black voids before. Morning was on its way, and with it came a resounding hope. Trudging through the woods in the pitch black was highly overrated and absolutely not recommended. I hoped to never have to do it again. For any reason.

It was the subdued sound of trickling water that reminded me of the task ahead of me. The narrow stream of water at my feet continued along the muddy bottom of the trench. The diminished volume of the stream, along with the sound of only an occasional drip on the leaves overhead, told me the rain had all but stopped. Even though it was shallower and flowed slower than it had before, the stream was still leading the way.

Likewise, I was relieved to find that the sharp pain in my ankle was all but gone, too, having been replaced by only a throbbing ache. It was still painful, but at least manageable. At this point, it looked worse than it felt. Shades of blue and purple painted the lower half of my leg like oil on canvas, and for some reason, the sight of it filled me with sadness. Swollen and cocked at just enough of an angle to look anything but normal, I could tell it was messed up. Badly. And if not treated properly, it may never be the same. But, then, what part of me ever would?

And I was lucky.

The image the long bone sticking from Becca's eye socket snuck up on me like a rapist and I wondered how long it would take to erase the vision from my mind. With a deep inhale and equally substantive exhale, I prepared to move out. I'd been incredibly lucky getting through the night undetected. But, I also knew it would only be a matter of time before the psycho found me and it would mean a death sentence if he did. Regardless of what I had hoped, I knew he wouldn't just give up. He couldn't afford to. The desperate look in his eyes back in the basement told me that. And down here in the crevice, there was nowhere to run and nothing more than the empty beer cans to protect me.

After relieving myself into the already trickling rainwater, I pulled my phone out to check for service once more and wasn't surprised by what I found. What I wouldn't give to hear my mother's voice right now. Or my father's. I would generally do whatever it took to escape their inquisition, but right now, I'd take it. I'd enjoy it, in fact. I'd listen to every word with rapt attention and agree with anything they said, just to hear them again.

Using the muddy walls of the trench for support, I started making my way down the hill, following the water that flowed along the bottom. It was slow going, but the walls provided a great support system, and I was able to cover more ground than I would have if I were topside. The quicksand-like mud occasionally sucked down my feet, like it didn't want me to leave, but I didn't let it stop me.

I slopped through mud and sludge, making my way toward a lake that had eluded me in the night. As I did, two significant things began to happen. First, the trench grew more and more shallow, concealing me less and less the farther I moved along. As my eye level rose higher and higher above the top of the trench, I started feeling more and more vulnerable. But, that vulnerability was tempered by the fact that I didn't have much farther to go. It was like a deadly race, with nothing short of my very life on the line, trying to make it to the finish line before being cut down by a sadistic killer.

The second thing I noticed was that it was definitely getting brighter. The occasional glimpses through the treetops revealed a sky that was no longer black, but more of a dark, charcoal grey. Ashen clouds churned busily as they rolled overhead. Dawn was indeed coming, but it wasn't going to be a bright, sunshiny morning, that was for sure. Too bad, too, because I could have used a little sunshine.

Bone 50 White

Sand spread out before me like a welcome mat. A dirty, brown pock-marked welcome mat. Lying just beyond it, the steel blue water of the lake. My chest swelled as I took in a relieved breath of air. I couldn't help but smile, and I almost started crying all over again. As excited as I got whenever Garrett and I explored a new lake or river, I'd never been so happy to see a body of water. If my ankle hadn't been so messed up, I would have broken into a run at the very sight of the water, diving right in to wash away all the built up grime and fear. Cleanse my mind and body of everything I'd seen back at the church.

Instead, I cautiously limped out of the woods and onto the beach, taking a quick look around as I did. The good thing about the beach was that it was empty. No psychos. The bad thing about the beach was that it was empty. No sign of anyone to help. Really, no sign of life period. Not even a squirrel or bird. It was as if someone had hit the "delete" button on any and all life in the area.

The overnight rain and what had probably been years of neglect had firmly packed the coarse, wet sand. It was obvious no one used the beach any longer. Small groups of teens looking for a few unsupervised hours in the sun might come by and hang out now and then. An occasional fisherman might cut across on the way to his favorite spot, but that was probably it. Kids no longer built sand castles, or buried their brothers or sisters. No mothers were lying on colorful beach towels reading light summer novels as their means to get away. And no young men were spending their afternoons trying to conceal their budding erections as they applied suntan lotion to their bikini-clad girlfriends.

Without a doubt, the beach had seen better days.

Now, stray tufts of weeds and grass poked through the sand like acne. An old yellow nylon rope, probably used to section off the shallow area, lay half buried in a line snaking from one end of the beach to the other, the attached red buoys faded from years of summer sun. A blue plastic container lay discarded and empty, the bait that had come in it having long ago become fish food. All combined, they were sad blemishes on what was once probably a great family summer spot.

And then there was the snack shop. My heart skipped a beat when I first turned and saw it perched atop the small hill between sparse stands of pine. Its appearance resembled much of the beach it overlooked. Like it had been abandoned for years. The outside of the building hadn't fared much better than the church I had escaped from, and that sent a cool shiver through my blood. Pink paint was peeling off the concrete blocks in strips, waving gently in the breeze. Several of the windows had been broken out, and the end of the gutter on the side facing the lake drooped almost to the ground on one end, its supports having rusted through with age. Sun-bleached cardboard advertisements for soft pretzels and Slush Puppies hung cockeyed on the windows that hadn't yet seen a rock from a vandal's hand. An equally washed out red, white and blue

Pepsi sign swayed gently in the breeze. The words "Tall Pines Ice Cream and Snacks" were painted in blue at the bottom and like the building itself, the sign's white paint was also chipped and peeling, revealing a pale grey underneath.

With my ankle bitching about the difficult walk down the trench, I turned my attention back to the water and tried to decide my next move. I couldn't see much of the lake itself, so I hobbled and winced my way down to the water's edge. There, gentle waves lapped up onto the sand like they were trying to eat as much as they could before retreating.

I looked to the left, toward the sandy patch where we had stashed Garrett's boat. In the weak light of the dawn, I saw a tiny patch of sand several hundred yards down the shoreline through trees that jutted out over the water separating the two beaches. Just the sand, not the boat, but I was sure it was the same stretch. My heart leapt into my throat and I cautioned against my excitement getting the best of me. Garrett must have made it back to the boat and was well on his way to get help.

But my excitement was premature after all. A subtle breeze swayed the tree branches and exposed a flash of dark blue aluminum hull. The $200 boat we'd restored a couple years ago was solidly in place. Right where we'd left it.

I quickly curbed my sudden discouragement, reminding myself that this meant the boat was there for me to use. This was actually a good thing. Not as good as Garrett getting help, and it would be more than a little difficult getting through the stretch of densely wooded, hilly land between me and the vessel, but it was better than nothing. Between the beaches, the shoreline became a sheer cliff, dropping straight down at least ten or twelve feet to the water. Not the best terrain to navigate for someone in my condition. In fact, it would have been a difficult hike even if I had full use of both my legs. But, then again, I'd never been tested like this before.

I looked back out over the lake, hoping to see a light from a boat, a dark shadow on the water, something. But, there were none. The thin mist that hovered above the gently rolling water was unbroken. Nobody was on the lake yet. It was still too early, but I knew the mindset of a fisherman. Being a Saturday morning, someone would be coming by at some point. I just hoped that whoever showed up wasn't the man with the bolo knife.

Fresh blood was seeping through my sock, urging me to rest my ankle again. I needed to sit down, take some weight off it, but I really didn't want to be sitting out here in the open while I waited for a boat to come by. I was already feeling vulnerable just standing out by the water's edge without any cover. I looked back up at the snack shop and shivered from the early morning chill against my bare skin. With its broken windows, I'd be able to hear a motor before it got too close. That would certainly give me enough time to hobble out and wave them down.

What the hell.

I'd give it a half hour or so, and if nobody came by, I could always get in the water and try to make my way along the rocky shoreline to the boat. It would be treacherous, but what hadn't been over the last twelve hours or so? Even if I didn't have the energy to paddle the boat very far, simply shoving off and floating out into the water might be better than staying here. I would definitely be out in the open and vulnerable then, though the one thing I had in my favor was the man's weapon of choice. The bolo knife. A weapon like that required a face to face encounter in order to use it, and I was sure I could make that difficult out on the water, broken ankle or not.

I turned and started limping up the narrow path that led up the slight hill to the snack shop. There was as much grass growing in the disappearing path leading up to the small concrete-block building as there was on the beach. With apprehension already settling into my chest, I could only imagine what kind of condition the inside of the building would be in.

Bone **51** White

She wondered if the boy knew the woods as well as she did. Doubted it. If he did, then he would have most certainly used one of the hiding spots that she knew of, and she hadn't found him in any of them. As it was, he could be anywhere, and that meant the questions were coming faster than she could answer them. In fact, she didn't have any answers at all. What direction was the boy going? Was he heading toward the road? Making his way to the lake? Or was he going in another direction entirely, one that wasn't so obvious?

She also wondered if her father had gotten out of the church soon enough see which direction the boy had gone? Or if he was searching as blindly as she? This led to her wondering where her father had looked and where he was now. She might not be smart, but she knew it wouldn't do any good to search where he already had. Unless the boy had backtracked, of course. He could have gotten turned around in the darkness.

Her brow furrowed, and the familiar pain behind her left eye was making a comeback. Always did when she was thinking too hard. And tracking the boy down was proving more difficult than she had thought.

In swift arcs, she used the hatchet to clear a path in front of her. Not because she had to. The brush wasn't all that thick. She simply wanted to. She wanted to sever the brambles and force them to die at her feet. She marveled at how effortlessly the blade cut the small branches, like it was slicing through nothing but the early morning fog. She silently thanked her father. He always kept his tools sharp. A dull blade made the work more difficult, he always said. Keep it sharp and let the blade do the work for you. Now she understood.

Her anger at the boy hadn't subsided. If anything, it had only intensified over the last hour. Tromping through the wet forest had left her waterlogged, cold and miserable. So with each sapling that fell by the wayside, she imagined it was the boy falling to the soggy ground, cut down by her own hand. And the pleasure she got from it quieted the pain in her eye.

Lately, she had been wanting more and more to help Father with his work. Fantasized about it really. The smell of his work clung to him and would hover in their room after he would leave her. After she was done being a woman for him. It would linger in her nose, and once she was sure he was gone, she would do that thing. That thing she didn't need him for. All the while, dreaming of doing the work. The screaming. The blood. The sounds of the lawnmower blade hacking away at meat and bone. The desire always left her body trembling and her sheet damp.

Sometimes afterwards, as she gave her heart a chance to calm itself and allowed her breathing to return to normal, she wondered what her mother would think. Would she be proud? She didn't think so. She didn't think her mother would be proud of her at all. Father hadn't had the time to teach Mother the way he'd taught her. If he had, then maybe. Surely then, Mother would be proud.

But now, the only parent she had left, the one whose praise she craved, was her father. And this was her chance to show him. Show him that not only did she have the desire, but she was capable. She could make the boy dead. Section him off. Harvest him. Do all the work that needed to be done.

Father would be proud. At first, he would be angry with her for leaving the church, but then he would be proud of the great job she had done. She did not think he would punish her this time. Definitely not this time. He couldn't. Not if he saw that she had been a good helper. A good pupil. Not if she caught the boy. Not if she cut him down like a sapling.

Bone 52 White

Luckily, the door to the snack bar wasn't locked. In fact, there was no door, just an open space where the door had once been. Cautiously, I stepped through the opening and took it all in.

Everywhere I looked, remnants of a once thriving business lay in ruin. Short stacks of white Styrofoam cups had toppled like bowling pins across the waist-high countertops. Dingy and water-stained napkins littered the cracked linoleum floor haphazardly, yet completely, scattered by the wind blowing through the broken windows. A tall stainless steel freezer had once gleamed brightly, but it now leaned solemnly in defeat, riddled with a million tiny divots. Buckshot. Four separate pieces of a metal window frame lay next to a pane of glass on the counter that separated the front area from the back. It looked as if someone had plans to replace the window before giving up and leaving it behind.

Unfortunately, not everything in the place was from the business side of things. A soiled pair of pink panties, ripped, as far as I could tell, lay on the floor beside the counter. I wasn't sure what it was until I saw the purple condom wrapper crumpled beside them. It was obvious, then, what had taken place. I wasn't sure if it had been consensual or not, but decided to ignore the possibilities. Scrunching up my nose, I walked further in, kicking aside small piles of napkins and wrinkled leaves left over from the Fall.

Despite glass missing in many windows, a heavy, pungent odor hung in the air. Its rankness was one that had become all too familiar during the previous night: the smell of rotting flesh. I remembered it coming from the calf's head Garrett and I had found in the creek, but was more closely associated with the church's basement, only this was worse. More rancid. The nauseating stench was about as welcome on my already queasy stomach as a bucket of pig intestines left out in the sun. I turned the corner and went down a short aisle toward the source.

The girl's restroom was a nightmarish scene. It looked like someone had performed an impromptu science experiment. A dissection gone horribly wrong. Splayed out in the middle of a sticky black puddle lay some sort of unfortunate animal. It could have been either a beaver or raccoon, but the carcass was too decayed to make out any discernible traits. The matted hair had turned black from the dried blood that covered every inch of the animal. The limbs had been cut free from the body and laid neatly beside it. There was no tail that I could see, but that didn't mean there hadn't been a tail at one time. From the looks and smell of it, the remains had been there for quite awhile.

Holding my nose with one hand, I reached in and pulled the door closed with the other. But not before having to kick out the wooden doorstop that seemed to have been put there with a sledgehammer. In all actuality, the pool of thick blood had spread its way to the edge of the open door and literally glued the doorstop to the floor.

With the door finally shut, I let out the breath that I'd been holding for the last twenty seconds. The breeze coming through the windows should certainly air the place out. Although, with any luck at all, my stay at the abandoned snack shop would be a short one, and I wouldn't have to endure the odor for long.

Feeling fairly optimistic that I'd lost the killer somewhere in the wilderness, I found an area up front that was relatively clean and grabbed a seat on the floor. And by clean, I mean clear of panties, condoms and dead animals. I sat with my back against the wall, eyes closed, listening for the sounds of activity on the water. Actually, any sound at all. From the lake, the woods or otherwise. I rubbed my ankle, trying to massage out the pain, but it only seemed to make it worse. In the time since I'd left the trench, the pain had been coming and going, alternating between a sharp pang and a dull throb. Right now, the sharpness was back, making its presence felt, and the cold chill in the air wasn't helping.

I stretched my leg out on the floor and allowed my head to rest against the cool concrete wall. In the silence, my mind drifted, wandering the halls of my recent memories, before eventually getting around to Becca. It was inevitable. I'd been putting it off, trying not to think of her at all, for fear of what might come out. But, I couldn't do it any longer. I would have welcomed any happy thoughts, warm memories of her. But at this point, there was no place left in my fragile mind that could segregate the good from the bad, so I'd tried to block them all out instead.

Now, try as I might, I found that one image kept intruding, pushing its way to the front of the line. It was her eye staring at me as I lay on the basement floor. No matter how much I forced myself to imagine her as she was before, it was that image that kept coming back. The bone, white as snow, sticking out of her eye socket like an arrow. Pointing at me. Accusing me. Reminding me that I had failed her.

No. It was *his* fault, not mine, but I wasn't entirely convinced. For the second time since I'd left the church, tears formed in the corners of my eyes. This time I didn't even try to stop them. This time I let them flow freely down my cheeks, as I gave in to the shudders that wracked my body.

Bone 53 White

The sound of footsteps on the linoleum brought me out of my reverie, catching the air in my lungs. My head snapped up, but I wasn't quick enough to make the first move. A man was standing in front of me before I even had the chance to flinch. I started to scoot away before recognizing him, or not recognizing him was more accurate. It was *a* man, but not *the* man. Some of the air escaped my lungs, and my nerves settled slightly. I quietly cursed myself for letting down my guard a second time. I was pushing my luck, and couldn't help but wonder how long it would hold out.

This man wasn't nearly as large or as young as the derelict thug from the church. Dressed in rugged khakis, grey flannel shirt and brown hiking boots, this man could have easily been my grandfather. An old floppy fly-fishing hat hid what looked to be thinning white hair, while shielding the kind, hazel eyes peeking out from an impressively thick and equally white beard. He had a universally familiar air, like he was not only somebody's grandfather, but probably a damn good one.

I scrambled from the floor, hampered by the inability to put much weight on my ankle.

"Whoa, it's alright, son," the old man said, his arms outstretched in a calming manner. "Sit. Sit."

But I was already up and leaning my back against the wall. With filthy hands, I started to wipe the dampness from my eyes and cheeks, an optimistic grin tugging at the corners of my mouth. I wanted like hell to think positively for once, relieved that I was no longer alone. The old guy seemed harmless enough, but more than that, he was the kind of old man anyone would feel comfortable turning to for help. But, after the night I'd just had, my senses were still somewhat alert. Maybe they always would be.

"Name's Henry Allen," the old man said, letting his hands drop to his sides. He stepped closer, stopping just short by a couple feet. "Was fishing off the bank up there a ways. Saw you out on the beach, not getting along too well. Thought I'd come and see if you needed some assistance."

I offered a poor attempt at a smile, but just couldn't pull it off. I was happy to see him, though I'm not sure the same could be said for the old man. The more he looked me over, the more his eyes narrowed. The warmth in his features cooled and growing concern put a crease his brow. I detected a change in the winds.

"Now that I got ya close up, uh, I'm seeing you got more wrong with ya than a hurt leg." He nodded toward my arm. My eyes followed his gaze, and drawing my arm in front of me, I saw what he was seeing. My shoulder and the entire right side of my shirt were covered in blood, Becca's blood, drying to a deep burgundy. The sight of it was like a knee to the groin.

"You in some sort of trouble, son?" The inflection in his voice told me at least some degree of skepticism had entered his thoughts. I couldn't quite blame him, considering the condition he'd found me in. He was probably wondering if he should even be getting involved, and there was nothing I could say that would erase that doubt. At least nothing short of a lie.

I pulled my eyes away from the blood and looked the old man straight in the eyes. I wanted to tell him everything. Let it all out. The horror. The fear. The whole fucked up story. But, I didn't feel like we had the time. A story like the one I had to tell couldn't be told without prompting a hundred questions. The fewer questions I had to answer, the sooner we would get out of here. And the sooner we got out of here, the better. So for the time being, I thought it best not to even mention that the blood wasn't mine.

"You have no idea," I said, shaking my head. "We need to get out of here. Now."

"I got my truck parked up the shore a ways," he said, gesturing toward something beyond the snack shop's walls. "About a hundred yards or so. Pretty thick bush between here and there, but there's an old fisherman's trail that cuts through. If you think you can make it to the truck, I can get ya to a hospital. 'Bout twenty minutes from here."

"I can make it," I said, pushing off the wall and stepping toward him. Hell, I'd made it this far. What was another trek through the wilderness at this point? At least this time I'd have an actual destination to get to, and wouldn't just be wandering around aimlessly. I'd have a guide and a path, just as long as our path didn't cross the killer's.

Having decided I could walk on my own, Henry turned and started for the door he'd come through, not even waiting for me. There was an anxiousness in his manner now. A sense of urgency.

"Do you have a cell phone?" I asked, using the countertop for support as I followed my new best friend like a puppy dog. Maybe his phone would be better. Or, at least his service.

"No," he said. "No, I don't. The grandkids are always telling me I need to get one, on account I'm getting' so old and spend so much time out here by myself. But, I think they're just afraid I'm gonna up and die out here one day and nobody'd ever find me." He chuckled, but I didn't get the joke. In fact, death was probably something I would never find humor in again.

Henry was a couple of steps from the open doorway when he stopped abruptly, then took a startled step backward. He nearly ran into me and I stumbled back a step myself.

"Well, hello there, friend," Henry said, with that same grandfatherly chuckle. "You startled me."

Alarms went off in my head, because I knew he wasn't talking to me. My heart rate shifted into overdrive, and the hairs on the back of my neck prickled. I leaned to the side to see who the old man was talking to. My stomach immediately leapt into my chest.

It was the man from the church.

The man who had killed Becca.

The man who had followed me all this way to kill me.

Bone 54 White

The raincoat was too big on her, and the hood hung down almost over her eyes. She'd been fighting with it all night, but the rain had finally stopped. She slipped the jacket off and draped it over a large rock where she'd be able to find it later. It felt good to be rid of the extra weight. But now, the leftover rain clinging to the shrubs and tree limbs was slowly dampening her sweatshirt. Soon, it would be saturated. Then she would be, too. Soaked to the bone. Still, it felt better without the raincoat, and she didn't miss it one bit. Even the hatchet that had been growing heavy in her hand felt lighter now.

The new day had broken with still no sign of either the boy or her father. She had covered all of the woods between the church and the road, the direction she'd seen them both go. Checked all the places she would have hidden if she were on the other end of the hunt. She knew someone could only hide for so long. At some point, they would have to move on. She'd seen footprints here and there, places where it looked like someone had been, but she was no tracker and didn't know the first thing about using the information she was gathering.

She decided to head toward the lake, curl back around by the church and maybe search the woods on the other side. That is, if Father wasn't already home with the boy. Part of her hoped that was the case. A very small part of her. The part of her that had spent too much time cooped up inside the church and wasn't used to this much physical exercise. Then her miserable little hunting expedition would finally be over.

The rest of her hoped her father wouldn't be there. It would be bad for her if he was. Very bad. She had thought it would be worth the risk, if for no other reason than to prove herself to her father. But with her determination fading, taking her confidence with it, she wasn't so sure. Maybe she should just return home and wait. Pretend she'd never left. Sit in her room, continue reading her mother's books until the ordeal was over. But, that would mean missing a perfect opportunity to show Father she was ready to help. It might be the only one she'd have. The back and forth was all so confusing.

A low-lying tree branch grabbed the sweatshirt, ripping the seam along her shoulder. The gift from Becca ruined, she staved off the tears and stopped walking. Glancing around the damp woods that stretched unbroken around her, she questioned if maybe she wasn't as ready as she thought.

Bone 55 White

The man smiled at Henry, his grey crooked teeth jutting in all directions like headstones in a forgotten cemetery. It was the kind of smile used for greeting an acquaintance, someone you knew in passing. Not overly friendly, but pleasant enough. The smile seemed even more surreal, like a scene from some dark anime, when the sword-like bolo knife appeared in the man's raised hand.

As the knife made its descent, Henry put his arm up to deflect the blow, only to lose it right below his elbow. The motion was swift and the severed limb dropped like a branch lopped from a tree, landing at Henry's feet with a sloppy thud. But the arm had done its job, and the knife swung wide of its originally intended mark.

The scream that came from Henry was like something out of a horror movie. Like nothing I'd ever heard. And knowing why and whom it was coming from made it all the more terrible. The guy had wanted to help me, out of sheer goodness. And look what he'd gotten for his compassion.

I was stunned at the rapid turn of events. But Henry didn't even hesitate. Before the shock had a chance to settle in, or his assailant had a chance to reload, Henry lowered his good shoulder and rammed the man in the stomach, driving him into the wall just beside the doorway. The old man's strength was surprising and inspired me to help him somehow. Two against one. We had a chance.

I swept my hands across the cluttered countertop for something to use as a weapon. A discarded knife would be good. A two-by-four would be better. My eyes came to rest on the broken steel window frame. The pieces weren't much, but with nothing else around, they were everything. I launched myself toward them, ignoring the protest from my ankle. Gripping the thin piece of metal defiantly in my fist, I turned back around, just in time to see the long bolo knife enter the small of Henry's back. It sank deep into the meat pillow of Henry's body. All eighteen inches of honed steel disappeared into the growing balloon of red on the back of Henry's grey flannel shirt. I watched in horror as the tip of it pushed its way through his abdomen, emerging just below his ribcage. The strength that had been so inspiring only seconds before was instantly sapped. Henry slumped to the dirty linoleum in an agonizing death he didn't deserve.

You know those little whirlpools that appear when the last of the water is draining out of the bathtub? A moment before, my tub had been filled to the brim with confidence. But that bolo knife had just pulled the plug as easily as it had sliced through Henry. And the last of my bravery was going down the drain.

In the seconds that followed, a million thoughts raced in my head. Without Henry, the numbers advantage was gone. And having just witnessed the bolo knife's capabilities, my piece of window frame, while sharp and pointed at both ends, would be useless in comparison. I downshifted out of fight gear and into escape mode, mentally mapping the layout of the small building. I wanted to drop everything and just run, but with him being so close and it being light out, there was no way I was going to lose this guy in the woods again. Not this time. Especially with my bum ankle.

Out of nowhere, the image of something I had seen outside popped into my head. A broken flagpole lay alongside the front wall. Where it once proudly flew the American flag on summer holidays, it now lay severed in sections the size of baseball bats. Handy, manageable baseball bats. And that became my plan. Fight back *and* escape. But, I had to move fast if I was going to get to them before he got to me.

The man had a foot on the back of Henry's neck and was effortlessly retrieving his weapon as I dashed around the corner into the hallway where the restrooms were located. I was actually doing more limping than dashing, but I was going as fast as I could. I remembered a third door at the end of the hallway, red with a black 'Employees Only' sign posted on it. It must lead to the snack shop's storage area and I was counting on a rear exit. Hopefully, if I had any luck at all, I wouldn't have to outrun the man for long, just long enough to get around to the front of the building.

I passed the blue door to the men's room, then the women's door that concealed the animal remains. The caustic smell hadn't dissipated by much, but I didn't stick around long enough for it to get to me. Besides that, foul smells had become a staple of this little excursion. The hallway seemed longer than it had moments before, like I was in one of those classic black and white films where the camera stretches out the hallway to three or four times longer than it really is. As I kept going, the red door at the end of this hallway was doing just that, moving away with each step I took

My left ankle threatened to buckle every time I put weight on it, but I kept moving until my shoulder finally slammed into the red door at the end of the hall. The rusted hinges gave way without hesitation and I tumbled into a storage room. At least, it had been at one time. Now, it was empty. Metal shelves stood bare alongside one another against the far wall. Broken cardboard boxes formed a tiny mountain in one corner, their sides ripped open and their contents long since pirated. Still, the room had exactly what I needed: a back door. Or rather, a back doorway. Just like the front, the door was missing, and nature was making itself welcome.

Pausing for only a fraction of a second, I skirted my way through a sea of dried orange and red leaves that crunched underfoot. Once I was framed in the doorway, I waited, my chest rising and falling, pulsing with adrenaline, until I could make out the sound of hurried footfalls on linoleum. He was following me down the hallway just as I hoped he would. It was the daring part of my plan. He had assuredly noticed my injured leg as I limped away, increasing his confidence in his ability to catch me. I was counting on that overconfidence to save my life.

Just through the doorway, something strange caught my eye. Something I hadn't seen up to this point. In the middle of the woods directly behind the building was a clearing. Small in comparison to the one at the church, a mostly dirt parking lot spread out with an equally overrun road leading from it into the woods. Both had been overtaken by weeds and grass and were barely visible. Both had also turned to mud overnight. I thought of the possibilities. Then almost immediately, I thought of my bum leg and remembered how long Garrett and I had walked along the old road the night before. How sparsely populated the area was. Henry's truck was a sure thing, but getting there on my bum leg wasn't. The flagpole was a probability at best, but I was more likely to reach it alive than the other side of the parking lot. I needed to stick with my original plan.

Footsteps echoed through the doorway, and I turned to the right, forcing my way through dense brush and thicket toward the front of the building. There was no more running. Even if my ankle would allow it, the density of the brush wouldn't. As I pushed aside a tangle of something that smelled like honeysuckle, a flash of doubt entered my mind. Perhaps I was wrong about the downed flagpole. Maybe I'd conjured it out of thin air due to the lack of another worthy plan. But, it was too late to worry about that. It had to be there. There was no turning back, and I couldn't let doubt slow me down.

It wasn't until I was rounding the corner to the front of the building that I risked a quick glance behind me. The timing couldn't have been better. The man had just come through the doorway, and in that instant, he saw me, too. Our eyes met for the first time since I'd escaped the basement. His hatred and desperation hadn't lessened in the time since he knelt on the floor holding his head. His intentions were apparent as he turned in my direction.

"For the hour to reap has come!"

"Bullshit!" I shouted, preparing to head for the corner of the building. The brush barely slowed him down, making me wonder if I'd have time for my plan. But I needed to fight the urge to take off. Going against every voice in my head, I needed to let him get closer.

"For the harvest of the earth is fully ripe!" he cried, brandishing the bolo knife for me to get a good look at. Then his face twisted in a deranged smile. "I've got customers waiting."

His words ran cold through my veins as I slipped around the corner. Thankfully, the broken flagpole was right where I'd remembered. I snatched up one of the three foot long pieces of steel tubing and tested the weight of the steel in my hands. I could feel the tables turning. I suddenly felt strong. Powerful.

Truly, and finally, able to defend myself in a way I never had before.

The sound of heavy footfalls drew closer and I took a deep breath. This was it. Now or never. One moment to determine the rest of my life. Gripping the section of flagpole like a baseball bat, I readied myself at the corner of the building, harnessing the adrenalin that was now pumping through me like vapors through a steam engine.

At the first sight of the man coming around the corner, I inhaled deeply and swung for the fences. Like a pro, I twisted at the waist. Opened my hips. Funneled all my strength down into my lower back and caught the man right below the ribcage.

The blow separated the oxygen from his lungs in a single, massive eruption. With it came a grunt, low and guttural. As he doubled over, the bolo knife slipped from his hand and landed on the carpet of pine needles. With both arms folded completely across his abdomen, he gasped for air. His knees hit the ground with a dull thud, giving him the posture of someone kneeling in prayer. But his eyes were stretched wide with panic and desperation.

I stood motionless, unsure what to do next. Was it enough? Was the objective only to buy myself some time, or to make damn sure he would never follow me again? The decision taking less than a second, I raised the pipe high in the air. With all my strength, I brought it down on the back of the man's head. The base of his skull exploded in a blossom of red mist that sprayed onto my face, warm and tacky. The sound it made was sickening. I was at once repulsed at my viciousness, yet energized by the feel of it coursing through my veins. He fell forward and rolled to the side, curled up as if he were simply a child going to sleep.

The section of flagpole dropped from my trembling hands as blood leaked from the man's wound. The puddle of red oxygenated liquid surrounded his ruined head like a halo as it spread out before seeping into the earth. The sounds from his throat ceased.

And in my mind, there was no doubt. He would never follow me again.

Bone 56 White

The scream stopped her dead in her tracks. She stood motionless, holding her breath, as her ears strained to detect the origin. Her wariness slowly turned to excitement as her mind worked to process the echo coming through the pines. The scream had come from down by the lake. Not too far from where she was. She rhythmically tapped the butt end of the hatchet against her leg, scouring her brain, trying to think of what might be in that area. Where could the boy have been heading? Had he been hiding somewhere? And when her thoughts eventually led to the old beach, she cursed herself for not thinking of it sooner.

Of course!

The beach had been closed for a few years, but she could remember spending time there when she was a little girl. It was one of only two real beaches on the lake, and her mother liked it because it was always less crowded, making it worth the added travel time, she'd say. A smile started to creep across her face when she thought of how they had gone there often. Just one of the many things they did. *Before.* Sharing blue raspberry Slush Puppies and soggy microwaved pizzas with new friends.

Sitting out on the diving board platform in the water, talking about boys and giggling when one would pull himself up out of the water with his butt crack showing. She'd even rolled down the hill and straight into the water, spinning inside a large, black inner tube, doing more bouncing than rolling. If she tried real hard, she could still smell the rubber.

Then there was the time, more recently, when her father had taken her there. It had already closed down. And he only took her there once. Just after they moved into the church. He'd been on edge. Angry. She remembered how rough he'd been. How much it had hurt. Her first time.

And just as quickly as it had come on, the smile faded. Not all thoughts of that place were happy ones. She didn't like thinking bad thoughts about her father. She scolded herself as she snapped out of her daydream, angry for wasting time just standing there. Father would have scolded her, too. And rightly so. This was not the time for reminiscing. Someone had just screamed. Screamed in agony and pain and a want to live. In her experience, that was a good thing. It meant work was being done.

Bone 57 White

Adrenalin still pulsed through me like a runaway wildfire as I leaned against the concrete building, assessing what I had just done. I'd killed a man. The very thought was both surreal and mind boggling. All of my pondering while in the coffin of whether I could do it seemed distant, like the thoughts of someone else. It was survival, I told myself. Anyone else would have done the same. Anyone else would have chosen to kill over dying. Maybe some would have stopped after the first strike, after they'd bought themselves enough time to get away. But who knows whether it would have?

I hadn't had time to debate and explore my options. I'd had to choose, and I chose the course that ensured my safety. It was a decision made out of both selfishness and righteousness. For everything I had seen and been through. For everything that man had done. For Henry. For Becca. There was no telling what atrocities this man had inflicted on people, the pain he caused. I'd killed him to make sure no one else would suffer. And I was merciful in doing so.

He deserved far worse.

My short breaths had just started coming at longer intervals when I heard two sharp beeps coming from the vicinity of my shorts. I pulled my forgotten cell phone from my pocket and flipped it open. The battery symbol in the middle of the shattered screen flashed red, and the tiny words below it said I had only two percent charge remaining. I almost chuckled. Like it mattered anymore. But then, reading through the cracks further, I saw something that pissed me off. I had four missed calls. The piece of shit phone hadn't even rung. My lips pursed and my jaw set tight. Thumbing through the list, three of the calls were from my mother, and the fourth was from Claire, who my mother probably called when she couldn't get ahold of me or Garrett. I wanted to throw the phone to the ground, smash it further into a million pieces, but another impulse ran through me. I weighed the phone in my hand.

The splash it made when I chucked the phone into the lake scared off a couple of lounging ducks. They took to the air, wings flapping in unison. And as I watched them fly off, I laughed. For the first time I could remember, I actually laughed.

"Fuck it," I said. "Fuck it all."

I inhaled deeply, filling my lungs with clean, fresh air. The fully risen sun had burned away the mists, leaving the color of the water, the beach, the sky, even the brown pine needles more vivid than they'd ever been. I turned to leave, and head up the trail to the waiting truck Henry had told me about, when my smile faded. I raised my face to the sky and silently thanked Henry for his sacrifice. Thanked him for trying. Thanked him for buying me time. I let him know that, with his truck waiting, Henry had helped me more than he'd ever know.

Bone 58 White

She stared down at the body, its vermilion blood spreading across the floor like spilled paint. This was the source of the scream. She didn't know the old man, had never seen him before. But, she knew her father's work. She knew what his knives did to the human body and how much blood they brought out. Her father had come this way, and that knowledge grew the seed of excitement in her belly. Excitement, and a little worry over running into him empty handed. Without the boy. She wondered if either of them were nearby.

The hatchet raised and ready just in case, she moved past what remained of the old man, cautiously side-stepping the blood engorged napkins that surrounded him. They looked like thin sponges, and she could imagine what would happen if she stepped on one. Thought about doing it, just to see, but decided against it. This wasn't the time for games. She followed the trail of bright red smears and dots that led away from the body, each one smaller in size than the previous. The trail led her around the service counter and down a short hallway where the drips tapered off in front of a pair of restroom doors.

The smell of rotting flesh greeted her, entering her nostrils. She nodded with a growing recollection. Even smiled a little through what was left of the anger and mounting exhaustion. As she breathed in the scent, basking in it, she savored the knowledge of a job well done. Foul smells were a comfort to her. One of the things she'd come to appreciate about her father's work. The smell was its own kind of reward. And this one even more rewarding because she'd brought it out herself. All by herself. This was her work.

It had been a couple months since she'd taken her first, secret step in learning her father's trade. He'd only brought her here the one time, but she'd come back to this building. When she'd tried to do his work. On a smaller scale, but still. It had been just as messy as his, that was for sure. But, a harvest was still a harvest, and she would always remember her first. Took great pleasure in it. It had been good practice. Especially since her first attempt hadn't gone as well. The cat had barely been seen since.

But this wasn't the time for reminiscing, either. Now was the time to continue her progression. To hunt down and harvest the boy. So she waved off the idea of looking in on her handiwork and concentrated instead on the other restroom door. The boy's restroom. The decision ahead of her caused her heart rate to bump up just slightly. Should she open the door? See what or who was on the other side? Make sure the boy, or anyone else for that matter, wasn't hiding in the tiny restroom?

The prospects of what she might find had aroused her curiosity. But, she also noticed the red door hanging crooked at the end of the hallway, and for some reason, it intrigued her more. Something had happened there. And by the looks of things, it was something violent. The sound of rustling leaves travelled from the room down the hallway, and she was relatively certain that either windows or another door were allowing the early morning breeze to come through.

The more she thought about it, if someone were hiding in the boy's restroom, they weren't going anywhere anyway. She could always come back. As she took the first steps down the shadowy hallway, she felt a flicker of pride in her growing investigative skills. They would most certainly serve her well in the future.

The back room was empty, and by the looks of things, had been for awhile. There were no signs of anyone. No more bodies, dead or living. Nothing that told her anyone had come this way, except a few kicked up leaves on the floor. She stared at them, the path cutting through the room barely discernible. The chirping of birds drew her eyes along the track to the open doorway on the back wall, and it was then that she realized her assumptions had been correct. Someone had definitely come through here. Her heart rate bounced with excitement. She was surprising herself with how well she was figuring out clues to the boy's whereabouts. So excited, in fact, that her anger had almost disappeared altogether. She even smiled. She was learning so much through this experience that she actually found herself grateful for the boys coming into her life and stirring things up. Maybe it was even a good thing.

With a clucking sound, she wasted no more time. She skipped though the storage room and out the open doorway into the woods. The first thing she noticed was the flattened brush that led along the side of the building. When viewed as a whole, it formed yet another trail. Without hesitation, and with a newfound spring in her step, she followed it.

Bone 59 White

I found the dirt path easier to navigate than the woods had been. And in the daylight, it was nothing like my struggles overnight. The well-worn passageway was more than a couple of feet wide with the grass trampled and all but gone. Henry had said it was mostly used by fisherman who parked their vehicles on the side of the road before cutting through the woods to the water.

Whether it was the numbness that had set into my leg again, or the huge weight that had been lifted from my shoulders, I actually felt light on my feet as I trucked along the path. For the first time since the prop had busted on the boat yesterday, things were going well. I was out of the hell I'd found myself in at the church, I'd killed the man who'd been trying to kill me, and with a truck waiting at the end of this path to take me home, I was starting to feel better. Maybe even a little cocky. I'd looked death square in the eye and walked away a winner.

The wind suddenly rustled through the trees tops, bringing with it a sound that not only froze my bold arrogance, but shattered it into tiny, jagged pieces. It came from behind me, back toward the beach. Part howl, part agonizing scream. Bordering on inhuman, but not entirely void of humanity.

Crazed was more like it.

And feminine.

I stumbled, falling into a cluster of white wildflowers and ivy. I grabbed onto a low-hanging tree branch to help me get back to my feet. A shiver started at the base of my spine, then played up my back like fingers on a keyboard. It had to be the daughter. The only person it could be. I had forgotten all about her, but apparently, she hadn't forgotten about me. She must have been searching for me, too, but had just found her father instead. Or at least what was left of him.

My pace quickened and I tramped toward the road, pushing my ankle to its limits and then a little further. The limits threatened to push back. As I ambled along the dirt path, I navigated the occasional raised tree root or fallen branch closely. The pain shooting up my leg quickly became nothing short of agonizing torture. But I didn't dare slow down. Even as the tears started to collect in the corners of my eyes, I pressed on. It was obvious that I had been wrong. Dead wrong. I was not yet safe. And my ordeal was far from over.

Bone **60** White

The mass of pulp was hardly recognizable; still, she knew it was her father. Face down in a pool of his own leaking blood. Didn't have to see his face. Just knew. She paced the ground beside the ruined body of the only family she had left, the butt end of the hatchet beating against her leg. The immediate throbbing quickly turned into a searing sting, but she didn't mind the pain. Didn't mind that it had cut through her pants leg and broken the skin, either. She used the pain for fuel. She was used to seeing blood, saw it all the time. Just not her father's blood.

She ran the fingers of her free hand through her thin hair over and over before eventually gripping onto what was there. The sight of the brutality waged against her father made her want to scream again. Scream and scream and never stop screaming until the anger was gone and her heart was empty. However long that took. With a guttural sound that came from somewhere deep within, she gave the fistful of hair a sharp tug, coming away with some of it between her fingers. Her heart was pounding, and her nerves were sizzling as if she was on fire. Perspiration enveloped her entire body, yet it failed to douse the flames that were burning her insides. She breathed heavily through her nose. Had to. Her clenched lips wouldn't allow air to pass.

Part of her wanted to cry. Cry, cry, cry the way she had for her mother. But, she couldn't give in to it yet. The tears couldn't come. Couldn't get through the rage that was swiftly consuming her, forcing all other emotions aside. There would be time for tears, but that time was later. Not now. Right now, she had to compose herself. Right now, there was work to do.

Now more than ever.

Her wild eyes searched the empty beach, then the lake. But there was no sign of the boy. Someone had done this to her father. Done it, and simply walked away like it was no big deal. It had to be the boy. Who else would have done it? No one. But, where was he? There were no boats that she could see, and no activity at all on the water. No sounds even. The morning air around her couldn't have been more still and quiet as she scanned the nearby trees. Where could he have gone? Then, finally, something caught her eye. And what she saw made her smile through the rage growing inside her. Something cutting through the thick mass of evergreens. Something that made the sun shine even brighter.

It was another path.

Bone **61** White

The rust-colored Ford waited on the graveled side of the road, pulled to the right just enough for vehicles to get past. Though, from what I'd learned of the area yesterday, it wouldn't be in anyone's way even if it was parked in the middle of the road. I didn't know if this was the same road Garrett and I had walked after beaching the boat, but it might as well be. And lord knows, we didn't see one car the whole time.

If we had...

The pickup itself was relatively new, and shone as if it had just been waxed. The morning mist had all burnt off, and the sun was catching the chrome grill enough to blind me if I looked right at it. Still, it was beautiful and I looked anyway. It was a sight for sore eyes. The first non-decrepit thing I had seen in days. I couldn't help but smile through my labored breaths, and wipe away the tears that had been leaving trails down my face. Set against the green wooded backdrop, the truck stuck out like a sore thumb. In a good way.

Garrett was a truck guy and would have fallen in love.

I barely managed to scramble my way up the steep embankment and onto the gravel roadside. I didn't even bother to look for traffic before I went around the front and over to the driver's side door. I could hear my mother's voice scolding me like a child, telling me to look both ways next time. *My mother.* My throat tightened at the very thought of her, and I realized that no matter how old a guy was, or how tough, when things go bad, we always want our mother.

In my rush to get as far away as possible, as soon as possible, I yanked too hard on the door handle and just about broke my wrist. It rose up slightly before coming to an abrupt stop. There was no disengaging sound, no rewarding click of the door opening. Shaking off the sting in my wrist, I jerked on the handle a couple of more times with my other hand, but got the same response.

The truck was locked.

Damn it! Why hadn't I thought about that? Why hadn't I checked Henry's pockets for the keys *before* walking all this way? I looked back in the direction I'd just come, back toward an abandoned snack shop, a Good Samaritan's dead body, and the killer I had killed with my own hands. And therein laid the answer to the question. I hadn't thought to check for the fucking keys, because I've never been through something like this! I was flying by the seat of my fucking pants, that's why!

Fuck!

My heart started pounding its cadence in my ears again. I couldn't believe I hadn't had a heart attack yet. My blood pressure had to be through the roof at this point, and I actually thought I could feel it swelling my brain. But that would be just my luck. After all I'd been through, all the narrow escapes, for me to drop dead beside this fucking truck on the side of the fucking road.

Fuck! Fuck! Fuck!

I wanted to let out a scream of my own. Just get it all out. But a voice told me it would be a very bad idea. It sounded like

Garrett's voice, but I couldn't be sure. Maybe Becca's, I don't know.

I emerged from my inner tantrum and knew what I had to do – go back to the snack shop and get Henry's keys. But, she was there, I reminded myself. And she was probably looking for me. But it was either that, or leave the truck behind and wander along the deserted road where she might also be searching for me.

I'd just looked across the hood toward the path I'd arrived on when the Ford's windshield exploded. Instinctively, I ducked at the first sound of breaking glass. I stayed down only long enough to hear the last of the shards tinkling onto the metal hood. When I rose back up, what I saw was way more ominous than a simple rock, or anything else I would have imagined if I'd been given three guesses.

The long wooden handle of a hatchet was sticking in the air, the iron head embedded deep in the glass. On the other side of the orange painted hood, stood the girl. *His daughter*. Her hands were wrapped around the handle of the hatchet, knuckles white as bone. Desperation and wrath twisted her features into something beyond ugly. Fury narrowed her eyes.

Frozen like an electric current had a grip on my muscles, I could only stand there watching as the girl struggled to pull the hatchet back out of the windshield. After a few hard tugs, she was cocked and reloaded.

Then she came at me.

I was slow to move, as if just coming out of a deep slumber. Even as she came around the front end of the truck, I just stood there, unable to make a decision. My mind was a blank slate. It wasn't until she cried out sharply as she lunged forward that I finally snapped out of it and started sorting through my limited list of options. I would never outrun her, that was for sure. And there was nowhere to hide. Ultimately, the decision became very simple. It came down to one option, and only one option.

Stand and fight.

The hatchet blade began its arc. Catching the silver glint out of the corner of my eye, I jumped backward just as the toe of the blade clipped the front of my t-shirt. I felt a breeze cut across my stomach, as I heard the hatchet embed itself, this time in the truck's side door. The razor-like blade drove a thin black slot into the pristine orange metal. Hobbling forward, I grabbed for the girl's arm, intending to separate her from the wooden handle. I'd break the arm if I had to. But, the sheet metal of the truck's door hadn't collapsed around the blade like the windshield's shatter-proof laminate coating. The small ax separated itself from the door panel on her first attempt.

I followed through with my lunge, throwing all my weight behind it, and speared her in the chest with my shoulder. I wrapped my arms around her like a linebacker making a textbook tackle. With my feet out from under me, the force of the blow sent us both hurtling toward the ground. All I could do at that point was hold on and make sure I pulled her down with me.

We hit the jagged gravel together, the impact forcing the air from my lungs. I gasped for the elusive breath as the blunt end of the hatchet banged off the back of my head, cracking against my skull. My grip on her loosened and we rolled apart. Stunned, I could barely get to my knees, fighting for every breath as I tried to orient myself. The girl, however, recovered faster than I did and scrambled to her feet before I could even get off all fours.

As the hatchet appeared against the light blue sky high above her head, a second tribal cry rose from her throat. Needing no further motivation, I dropped to my left and rolled away from her a half second before the hatchet made its downward arc. Once again, the blade failed to find its intended target, and the force of her swing momentarily threw her off balance. With her back turned, I pulled myself up, using the truck's polished bumper for support. Though technically on my feet, I was still doubled over with my hands on my knees, sucking air into my lungs in repeated gulps.

The low rumble came from somewhere behind me. It took a second for my oxygen-deprived mind to interpret the sound. A truck. And by the sounds of it, a very large truck. The mechanical growl grew louder, leaving only a matter of seconds before the truck thundered past. I needed to get the driver's attention. But the Ford was between us and the oncoming semi. Unless the driver just happened to look in his rearview mirror after he passed, he'd undoubtedly continue right on down the road, unaware that I was in the middle of a fight for my life. And that was unacceptable.

The girl's back was still to me and I watched her stumble as she tried to regain her footing. She must not have escaped the tumble unscathed, either. She was hurt. Dazed. With that knowledge in my back pocket, I seized the moment. Pushing off the hood of the Ford, I lunged at the girl, mindful of the hatchet this time. Coming up behind her just as she was about to turn around, I grabbed ahold of her dingy sweatshirt with one hand and a handful of dirty blond hair with the other. A scream escaped her. From pain, from rage, I didn't know which. And I didn't care. It took everything I had, every ounce of my diminished strength, but I was able to spin her in the direction of the road.

The harsh squeal of rubber against asphalt rang out as the driver saw the two of us. With white smoke erupting from the wheels, he braked hard, but the cement load it carried was too much for the truck to stop quickly. And when I used the very last of my remaining energy to shove the girl into its path, the front end with its stout bulldog emblem lifted her off her feet. She stuck there, plastered onto the grill for almost twenty feet until her body fell to the road as the truck slowed. With the last of its momentum, the rig rolled its large front tire over her, crushing the last bit of life from her body.

With my hands returning to my knees, the Earth began to shift on its axis. What was on my left went to the right. Right to the left. The ground buckled under my feet, and I staggered, trying to balance on a sheet of asphalt that waved in the wind. In the distance, I heard the labored creak of a door opening and someone yelling out. The voice came to me from the deep recesses of a tunnel. I stumbled backward until my back banged hard into the Ford, then I slid down against the tire and onto the rough gravel.

As I sat on the side of the road, resting against a damaged Ford truck, my mind drifted in and out. At times it was in the present, sometimes it was in the past and somewhere far, far off. In the sky above me, the trio of vultures that I'd seen the week before were back, circling gracefully overhead in their "wait and see" formation. They coasted effortlessly on the wind, and part of me longed to be that free. Gliding through the air. Out of reach. Bringing bad omens to others, while feeling none of the fear myself. Then, as suddenly as I'd seen them, the vultures were gone, and I was left to wonder if they had even been there in the first place.

I cocked my head just slightly and, out of the corner of my eye, I could just see the crumpled body of a girl lying underneath the truck. Lifeless. Beside the truck, a man bent with hands on knees, vomit spilling onto the asphalt.

And then a funny thing happened. Slowly, very slowly, the tension that had been gripping my shoulders and neck loosened. My body went limp without the support, and the rough gravel rose to meet my shoulder and arm. My eyes fought for closure, whatever the outcome. And this time, I let them. I finally welcomed sleep. I wasn't about to fight it. Not anymore. I was done fighting.

It wasn't long until a creeping blackness engulfed me, and my breathing slowed until only short gasps were coming out. The last thing I remembered was the sensation of someone shaking my shoulder, asking me questions.

What the fuck, buddy? What the fuck?

And the sour stench of vomit.

Bone 62 White

It was the feeling of being underwater, the dulled senses. Like when you're a kid in the pool, and you open your eyes while you're still beneath the surface. You look up and see the distorted figure of your mother standing at the edge. She's telling you that it's time to get out, that if you don't hurry, the flies are going to eat your PB&J. But underwater, you can't hear the actual words, only a low mumble letting you know that words are being spoken. Soft reverberations of sound waves traveling through the water and entering your ears. That's how it was for me. I couldn't make out the words, but I could feel reverberations all around me.

When I was finally able to pry my heavy eyelids open, the stark sunlight reflecting off the stainless medical equipment made me clamp them shut again. It was shockingly bright. Like coming out of the womb a second time. I heard a gasp, then a quick shuffle of feet just before the room seemed to retreat into darkness behind my eyelids. Carefully, I forced my eyes open again, and this time, found my mother's watery eyes looking back at me. Her flushed cheeks were raw and damp.

"Where am I?" I asked.

"You're in the hospital," she said, wiping the dampness from her cheek with a crumpled tissue that was obviously not fresh out of the box. "Oh, Luke, you're safe now, baby. You're safe now."

I grinned, or at least I tried to. I didn't know if it worked, but even the attempt exhausted me. My head sank back into the pillow and the warm embrace of my mother's love let me drift back to sleep.

When I opened my eyes again, I found my leg in the air, the sun streaming through the window behind three giant flower arrangements, and the room full of people. A doctor, several nurses, my parents, Cricket, Claire and George Stettler, the New Paris sheriff, all gathered around my bed, looking down at me with a combination of relief and pity. It was like the scene at the end of *The Wizard of Oz* where Dorothy wakes from her dream. Only the brainy scarecrow was missing. I didn't see Garrett anywhere.

"Welcome back," the sheriff greeted, peering down at me through wireframe glasses. His demeanor was tough, but kind. The wiry gray hair with the permanent indentation from his hat gave credence to the rumors that Sheriff Stettler was only a few months away from retirement. But he was on the job for now, so after telling me I had been in and out for two days, he got right down to business.

I answered his questions as they came, and the nodding of his head told me that I was mostly corroborating what they had already found out during their initial investigation. They had been awfully busy while I'd been out. Fifteen minutes later, he flipped his notepad closed, and sat back, but I had a few questions of my own.

"Are you sure you're up for this, Luke?" my mother asked, her eyes searching from the doctor to me with uncertainty.

"Yeah, Mom," I responded. "I can handle whatever the sheriff tells me. I lived through it, remember?"

She nodded tightly and clutched my hand, while my father escorted my friends to the hallway. Cricket turned on his heels and headed for the door like he couldn't wait to leave the room, but Claire shuffled her feet. I was grateful they left, though. This would be easier without having to see their faces.

"We'll give you some privacy. But he needs his rest," warned the doctor as he and the nurses turned to leave. "Don't stay long."

I sat a bit straighter in the bed and cleared my throat before addressing the lawman.

"Did you find Becca?" I asked. "Did you find her –"

My mother's grip tightened around my hand, and I witnessed my dad's arm snake around her for support.

"We did," the sheriff assured me. "Her parents have already made the identification."

The thought of Becca's mother having to go through that broke my heart, but I recovered from the thought quickly enough, determined to press forward.

"There's something I want to know," I said, looking Sheriff Stettler in the eyes. "I saw the boxes in the basement. That guy was shipping bones to people all over the world. Human bones. Who ... I mean, why ... or ..."

The sheriff held up a hand to end my pained search for the right question.

"Unfortunately, there are folks who buy bones, and I don't mean for lab specimens and what have you," he began. "Deviants with a human bone fetish. Goth musicians who think a human femur would look cool strapped to their microphone stand. Perverse individuals hide in all corners of the world, Luke, and unfortunately, they need to get their goods somewhere. It's the kind of business that can bring in a lot of money, as I understand from the FBI. They've been investigating a black market supplier somewhere in this area for awhile now. But it looks like you managed to pinpoint Mr. Barnes' operation."

"Barnes," I said, dropping my eyes to the sheet covering my lap. It didn't seem right to give him a name, like somehow that turned him into a person rather than the monster he'd been.

"Corwin Barnes," the sheriff continued. "Ex-con released from the penitentiary a couple years ago. Did a stretch for cruelty to animals. I'll never forget it."

"Cruelty to animals?" I asked, my mind still working a bit slowly.

"Like I said, I'll never forget it. He used to work at that church. Maintenance mostly. I guess some raccoons kept getting in his trash," the sheriff said, nodding his head and staring off into space. "Ol' Barnes finally set a trap and caught 'em all. The whole damn family. Only feedin' 'em poison or puttin' a bullet between their eyes was apparently too humane for that sumbitch. Guy was doin' all kinds of weird shit with the carcasses down in that basement. Skinnin' 'em, dissectin' 'em, making artwork and the like. Really sick shit. Anyway, we put him away for awhile, but it looks like he might have used prison as school. Bastard turned his sick obsession into a trade."

The sour look on my mother's face told me that she didn't care for where this conversation was going. So I changed the subject away from the gruesome stuff. I didn't see any reason to add to my mother's discomfort.

"This Barnes, he and his daughter actually lived there, didn't they? In the church."

"His daughter?" Stettler asked curiously. "Oh, you mean Belinda Turner. The girl hit by the cement truck."

"His daughter," I repeated. "That's what she called herself."

"She wasn't Barnes's daughter, although I suppose technically, she'd be his step-daughter," the sheriff continued after a thoughtful glance up. "Sixteen years old. Mother's name is Rosemarie, and we're trying to track her down now. Belinda's real father, Mr. Ellis Turner, has been deceased for almost nine years now. Killed himself when Belinda was only about four years old. Up and blew his brains out one day and the little girl was the one to find him in the bathroom. Most of him was slumped on the toilet, the rest was all over the wall beside him. A real mess, it was. Helluva thing. Anyway, the missus remarried Barnes shortly before we put him away for the animal nonsense."

"If it hadn't been for that connection, we wouldn't have even looked at the church," Stettler said.

"What do you mean?" asked my dad. "I thought you said that was where everything happened."

"That's where the bodies were, or what was left of them. Except for the girl's, of course. We responded to the cement truck accident. As messed up as she was, it was a nurse at the hospital who recognized her, but said she and her family had moved away a good year and a half ago. Couldn't find an address for Rosemarie Turner or a Rosemarie Barnes, and Barnes had skipped out on his probation. Honestly, we wouldn't have known anything about the murders if one of my deputies hadn't noted the proximity of Belinda's accident to the church where her stepfather had committed his earlier crimes. Well, when we put two and two together, we got four so we checked it out. Just walking up to the place we found blood on the porch. Fresh blood. Turned out, it was all through the church. Looked like a massacre took place in there. Even up in the loft. Thanks to DNA samples on file with the prison, they matched the blood to Corwin Barnes. After that, all the signs pointed to –"

"Wait," I interrupted, wondering if I'd either missed something or my fuzzy head just wasn't processing the information correctly. "How did his blood get all through the church? He's dead. His body's outside the snack shop by the abandoned beach. You'll find another body there. An old guy who tried to help me, but Barnes killed him. Henry something."

The sheriff's brow bunched, forming lines between his eyes. "Henry Allen. We searched the area and found him. But not Barnes. A lot of his blood was there, but not him."

A lump formed in my stomach despite the fact I hadn't eaten anything in two days.

"He's dead," I insisted. "I know it. I killed him." My body strained against the tucked in sheet, trying to rise from the bed. It was my father's hands that clamped down on my shoulders and held me back.

"Easy there, Luke."

I brushed one of his arms away, but stopped struggling. After a few seconds, I laid back in the bed.

After a long pause, the sheriff shook his head again. "I'm sorry son. We didn't find any body for Barnes."

"Then that means…"

"Okay, I think Luke needs to rest now," my mother pronounced, standing and holding her arm out to show the sheriff from the room.

"No, wait," I said, stopping them. "What about Garrett. Why isn't he here?"

My mother blanched like an almond and her eyes widened. She looked to my father for assistance.

"We can talk about Garrett later," he said, after exchanging a meaningful glance with my mother. "You need your rest."

I sat up in the bed again. "Well, I can't rest until I know how he's doing. I kept expecting him to show up..." I trailed off as pain filled both of my parents' faces. "He's ... he's okay, isn't he?"

"Luke," my father said, his tone stern yet comforting. But he didn't go on. Instead, he gave Sheriff Stettler a nod.

"We found him, Son," the sheriff said slowly. He removed his wire-rimmed glasses as he spoke, absentmindedly wiping them with a handkerchief. "Someone, presumably Barnes, had locked him in the shed back behind the church."

The shed. I'd run past it when trying to save my own neck. If I'd only known.

"How is he? Is he okay?"

You'd have thought that someone had painted a mural on the floor because everyone's eyes dropped to study it.

Sheriff Stettler eventually put his glasses back on and picked up his hat from the bottom of the bed, worrying its brim between his fingers. It was at that moment that I knew the answer. Knew it, but still needed to hear it, even as a thousand voices cried out in my head, all of them mine.

"I'm sorry, Son," the sheriff said, I could barely hear him over the outpouring of grief inside me. "If it's any consolation, he went quickly. The body was in a washtub, sliced from stem to stern. He would have bled out quickly."

"Garrett's dead," I mumbled, being the only one in the room brave enough to say the words. I repeated myself, this time with a bit more volume. I pinned my mother with my eyes as if making her face the reality of it. Swiveling in the bed, I faced Sheriff Stettler head on.

"Why?" I asked. "Why would someone do this? Do any of it? Just for fucking money? I don't understand!"

The sheriff's head wagged slowly back and forth. "Couldn't tell you for sure," he said. "Stuff like this usually comes from a combination of things. Abused as a child. Seeing others harmed. A life full of rejection. Maybe something in the family history. And then there's always the brainwashing power of plain old blinding greed. We may never know with Barnes," he said with a shrug. "The simple answer is that sometimes bad people go off to prison, and the system just fucks 'em up even worse. Pardon the French, ma'am."

My mother sat down on the edge of the bed, looking like she was planning to hug me. I wasn't the one she should be comforting. I didn't need her sympathy. I was the survivor of the whole ordeal. The only survivor.

I squeezed her hand and with a yawn said, "You're right. I need some sleep." When in all honesty, I just wanted to be alone.

Following on the sheriff's heels, my father led my mother out of the room, her head turning every couple of steps to make sure I was still there. She wore relief on her face like a mask, but there was still hesitation in her step. Hesitation to leave my side. I gave her a vague smile to let her know I would be okay, even if I didn't believe it myself.

Despite the setting sun through the window and the quiet that descended upon the hospital, sleep didn't come easy. Doctor's orders or not. I had too much on my mind. There were too many details, too many dead people occupying space in my head that weren't about to let me sleep. I'd lost too much. I lay awake as darkness descended, remembering every detail of my best friend as if fixing them in my mind would keep him with me. It was all I had left. Memories and tears.

Sometime during the night, a large vulture came out of nowhere and landed on the metal rail at the end of my bed. Its brown-black feathers interwoven and dusty, the scavenger hobbled over like it had been invited and hopped onto the wedge that held my ankle in the air. Its white head dipped up and down, picking at the cotton dressing wrapped around my ankle. I smiled at its antics, and decided to leave it be. It wasn't doing any harm.

Besides, I had the pretty young nurse to focus on. I wasn't sure when she'd come in, but she was efficiently checking my vitals when I first noticed her. It hadn't taken long to figure out that nurses couldn't care less if you slept or not, despite what they told you. At least once an hour, one of them would come in and poke around. They were constantly in and out of the room, checking this, emptying that. I expected this nurse to send my new friend away, open the window and shoo it right on out. But she appeared not to even notice it as she checked my pulse. I laid there with a thermometer under my tongue, watching her stare intently at her watch. Silently, her lips counted the beats one by one. She was tall with auburn-colored hair and soft skin, resembling Becca, my good friend from New Paris High School. Looked just like her, in fact, maybe older by a year or two.

With her firm fingers gripping my wrist just a little too tightly, she cast a sideways glance up at me and smiled with the same sweet smile I'd hoped to see on Becca's face when she passed me in the halls at school. A smile that said she was genuinely happy to see me. Then the nurse winked at me. And that's how I knew it was her. I feebly smiled back and laid there watching Becca go about a nurse's business, checking this, logging that, doing everything a real nurse would do. Where on Earth had she learned how to do all of it? And to think, I thought she was dead.

As I watched her, my heart rate started to rise. I could tell it was registering on her stethoscope, because Becca's smile slowly started to fade, and her forehead wrinkled slightly in puzzlement. I grew very cold, like all the heat in my body was being sucked out through the IV plugged into my hand. I could feel the sheets start to dampen beneath me, and the back of my neck grew cold. Still, my heart rate continued to climb and climb, to the point I thought my chest was going to split and expel my heart through the crevice.

My hands shot out to grab the bedrails, but they never made it, a tightness held them back. Looking down, I found my wrists bound, strapped to my sides by black leather straps with shiny metal grommets. They hadn't been that way before, and I looked to Becca for answers, my eyes full of fear. I wanted to beg for help, to plead with her to undo the straps.

But the nurse was gone.

Instead, standing beside my bed wearing a long white lab coat and glasses, was the man from the church. The man named Corwin Barnes.

The disguise didn't fool me. Neither did the compassionate and calming smile. I knew it was him, and I didn't even need to see the long, shiny bolo knife he held behind his back to prove it.

He stepped closer, resting a hand on the bedrail. My throat began to constrict, and it became difficult to breathe. My eyes started to water, and my vision blurred. But I could still hear. Unfortunately, I found I could hear just fine. And as he leaned over me, drawing his face and foul breath close, I could hear Barnes murmuring, practically whispering those words I would always remember…

For the hour to reap has come, for the harvest of the earth is fully ripe…

Nine Months Later

Epilogue

Dumbrăveni, Romania
(230 km NW of Bucharest, on the Târnava Mare River)

Arashk Dimir cradles the newly acquired brown package under his arm as he runs along the rain-saturated cobblestone of Mihai Eminescu Street Nr. 5. He passes the pink Hotel Marion where he works clearing tables when there are banquets to be hosted, performing maintenance when there are not. The road is empty on this late morning, save for the occasional car parked in front of the rows of pasty-colored houses. Neighbors, most of whom have known his mother since long before he was born, stand on their sidewalks or in their postage stamp yards tossing waves in his direction as he passes, yet Arashk pays them no mind. He's finally received his purchase. It took three weeks longer than the website had stated for delivery.

He can smell the garlicky fragrance of *ciorba de burta* before he even enters the apartment he shares with his mother. It is a comforting smell and he finds he is already anticipating lunch. At the front door, the key is hesitant to go into the lock, and he has to jiggle it just to get it started. He makes a mental note to oil the lock before he leaves the apartment again.

Entering the small kitchenette, he kisses his mother on the top of her head. "Bună dimineaţa, Mama."

His mother smiles and continues to stir the tripe soup that she knows to be her son's favorite.

Arashk heads directly to his room, and after shooting a glance back to make sure his mother's sometimes suspicious eyes aren't following him, closes the door. She's a wise woman and he loves her dearly, but she questions some of his interests. And of this one, he is certain, she would not approve. He sets the package on his bed and takes off his jacket, which he tosses onto the chair next to his makeshift desk of wooden crates and a slab of discolored bathroom countertop. The jacket slowly begins its descent, eventually sliding onto the floor in a heap. But he doesn't bother to pick it up. His eagerness won't allow it.

He perches on the bed, picks up the package and places it on his lap. It is not yet Christmas, and he's no longer a child, but he remembers the excitement of those mornings and it is similar to how he feels now. He'd saved nearly every *leu* he'd made working at the hotel over the last two months, minus the amount he gave his mother. He'd forgone *caffes* with girls, *Timişoreanas* with his friends. But, if his new purchase was indeed as the website described, it would be money well spent. And, hopefully, the first of many similar purchases.

The American vendor he had ordered from caused him a decent amount of worry, though, and he knew he was taking a chance. He had seen stories on the internet that services like it existed, but most of the people on the message boards swore they were only urban legends. Then, one day, a link had been emailed to the address he had setup strictly for browsing those kinds of message boards, and he'd worked up the nerve to give it a try.

Now, sitting on his bed with the subject of his fantasies securely in his grasp, he can barely contain his excitement!

The package's red, white and blue postage label was the first he'd ever seen and a trophy in and of itself. He had never before seen a package from America, much less received one personally. Pulling his father's pocketknife from his pants pocket, he decides he'll cut out the postage label and keep it as a souvenir. Keep it in the metal box under his bed, along with his father's ring finger that *Lupul* had sent his uncle after he'd been taken. The finger had arrived wrapped in a blue necktie with silver threading, *Lupul's* calling card, and that's just how Arashk kept it.

He starts at one corner and plunges the tip of the blade into the heavily taped package, mindful of not cutting too deep. Drawing the knife toward him, Arashk makes a slit the entire length of the cardboard box, then turns the carton around. With a slightly trembling hand, he does the same on this side until the top of the package is open on both ends. Impulsively, Arashk brings the box to his nose and breathes in deeply. The only smell he can detect, however, is the musty scent of old cardboard.

Being careful not to damage the postage label, Arashk works the knife in and out along the top of the box until the two flaps pop up in the center of the overstuffed package. His heart is pounding and he can't remember the last time he was this excited. Usually, the closest thing to excitement around Dumbraveni occurs when he and his friends make the two-hour trip to scare tourists seeking the remnants of a tired legend. He is always amazed at how many people actually believe that Dracula ever really existed. Especially Americans.

Arashk takes a deep breath, then lifts the flaps open until they hang outward, revealing a blanket of white Styrofoam inside. He smiles knowing his purchase is in there somewhere, nestled safely beneath the packing material. Slowly, he begins sifting through the tiny foam pieces in search of his prize.

Suddenly, his finger brushes against something hard, and Arashk jumps back, pulling his hand free as if afraid he'll be bitten. Just as quickly, he chuckles to himself.

"Imbecile."

Carefully, Arashk reaches back into the box, deep into the white foam and grasps the hard object. He lifts the item up slowly, spilling the Styrofoam pieces all over his lap and cascading onto the floor. When the top of the object finally emerges, like a ghost rising from the fog, a sharp intake of breath catches in his throat. It is the small, frail bones of a human hand, held fast to a varnished plank of wood with tiny silver wires. A young woman's hand, as promised. Brilliantly white. Delicate.

It is more beautiful than the website described.

More beautiful than he'd ever imagined.

* * * *

Blackened

A sequel to Bone White by
Tim McWhorter

Luke knows two unfortunate truths: sadistic killer Corwin
Barnes is still out there; and someday, he'll come calling.

A year ago, Luke put an end to Barnes's barbaric bone
harvesting operation, but it wasn't without consequence. With a
team of doctors, Luke has finally dealt with his heart-
wrenching losses and the heinous crimes he uncovered. He's
getting on with his life.

But his nemesis hasn't done the same, and Luke could never
imagine just how brutal Barnes can be.

Available Now